The Mysterious World
of Marcus Leadbeater

Ivan Southall

THE MYSTERIOUS WORLD OF MARCUS LEADBEATER

Farrar, Straus & Giroux

NEW YORK

To Francis Gordon Southall

1888–1935

CONTENTS

The Mysterious World
of Marcus Leadbeater

ONE

Leadbeater at the Outset

LEADBEATER, M. R. Answering to Marc. Year Eleven
student. Faintest light of the English class presided over
by Miss Gorgeous. The incredible, the ravishing Miss G.
Almost beyond credence, this lack of star quality, for el-
oquence seemed ever at the tip of his tongue.

How could this student, the principal asked, be so evi-
dent in class, yet effectively so absent? Though often dis-
figured by bandages, Band-Aids, and plaster casts, or
smelling of antiseptic dressings, nasal sprays, cough syrup,
liniments, or various herbal remedies for the relief of head-
aches caused by concussion. One hundred and ninety-two
centimetres tall—suddenly, and by surprise—and painfully
unaccustomed to it.

Phenomenal feeling for the stage. If judged by his age.
Numerous notable appearances since Year Six in the vi-
vacious company of the delectable Rosemary Richards,
supported, if not by a cast of thousands, then by eager casts
of several score.

Marc, a gift, not wholly of divine origin, to a generation

of generally frustrated schoolgirls. Marc mysteriously un-aware of the earnestness and promise of their interest. Re-markable failure to exploit his opportunities, considering the nature of his fantasy life.

Marc dragging through each day a great weight of virtue notably apparent to a majority of female students across the unusual spectrum of Years Seven to Twelve. Yet no-tably absent from the principal's periodic reports. ("Cannot make a basic computation." "Cannot write a grammatical sentence." "Rarely addresses himself to the question." "Not possible to equate his results in any academic pursuit with his family background.")

Marc, passenger on the 7:55 a.m. suburban train out of Melbourne Central, Australia, at the beginning of the first week of the third semester break. Intermediate destination attained at 9:05 for changing to the Peninsula bus. But at the instant of hurrying from the train (his haste established from years of habit), a thought:

"What's the rush? What's the panic? What's the point?" Hence stopping in the midst of the several passengers step-ping down with him.

Accidents of the kind being the norm. Marc, as always, accepting the injuries, the insults, and the blame.

A red-faced gentleman rubbing at his shins: "Bumble-foot. Tanglefoot. Idiot youth. Have you got rocks in your head?"

And the related complaint of an equally large lady de-scending upon his ankles with toes like chisels and heels like hammers. "Can't you tell your foot from your forefront? Are you soft in the head?"

Which made it just like any other place on any other day. Except in the good old times when Gramps was king

and Marc was clown prince and they were Leadbeaters
together.

"It's nothing, ma'am . . ."

"Nothing to whom? Are you looking for a clip on the
ear?"

"I'm sorry, ma'am. I really am. I know it's got to be my
fault. And it's not that I wasn't thinking, though I wasn't."

"You've got a problem!"

"True, ma'am, but I won't bore you with it."

"Gormless and helpless and witless and dumb. Can't
even get off a train."

"I'll be giving it serious thought, ma'am. I'll start applying myself to it very soon."

But I'm feeling sick, Marc thought. Sick to the gut. Sick
to the soul.

This is how it happens. Suddenly you've stood all you
can stand and you drop dead. Mum having coffee at the
Foreign Aid Club. Dad pushing some button in his Boeing
halfway to London. Beth and Jo Anne going through my
cupboards looking for what they can find that's no business
of theirs. Me lying dead, ghastly and anonymous among
strangers and trains.

Marc swaying. Perhaps turning green. Perhaps swallowing hard against a very nasty bile.

No one holding him up. No one standing by to care.
Everyone coming off the train having passed on to the spirit
realm. Nothing human left to be seen. Except for something
that appeared to be functioning as a ticket collector.

People, Marc thought, aren't what they were. When I
was a little kid and got sick on Sundays everyone was
stroking my hair and holding my hand and cleaning up the
disgusting mess.

Marc squinting up and down. Nothing the slightest bit disgusting to be seen. Except the ticket collector occupying the open gateway as if he were about to proclaim like Henry, King of England, on St. Crispin's Day.

"Yes," this character called, "it is I. The splendid, spectacular, and constantly vigilant one attired in bottle green. Am I to receive you with honour or the sternest accusations? Did you or did you not purchase your little piece of paper of the relevant colour from the ticket-vending machine?"

I've got a weirdo, Marc thought. Why does it always happen to me? Then reaching for his pockets with an attack of galloping insecurity. What little piece of paper? What relevant colour?

Oh my God. If I start rushing in circles waving my electric razor and tearing lumps out of my hair, he might think I'm homicidal and run for cover.

Marc searching his pockets with increasing desperation. No memory of any kind relating to a ticket-vending machine.

Marc protesting: "Tickets are immoral, mate. The railways belong to the people. And it stands to reason I couldn't have got on without a ticket. They wouldn't have let me through the gate."

The ticket collector acquiring a stern aspect and greater stature. "In your own hand, kid, and your own head, all secrets are hid. All knowledge of all goings and all comings and all arrivings. With or without a ticket. Just as in my hand I hold authority to dump you in the dungeon on dry bread and water. Here I stand, poised, symbol of an indignant body of bureaucrats, yet ready to collapse, amazed and grateful, upon the sighting of the colour of the relevant piece of paper."

So Marc said, "Start fanning yourself, mate. Collapse

heartily with gratitude and accept this crumpled bit of stuff from my hot little paw."

"I tender," said the ticket collector, "my sincerest thanks, for upon my soul if it does not bear the little hole commensurate with today's date. Thus assuring that the Met runs at a profit this week and the servant who waits upon you shall be paid."

"Everyone's a wit," observed Marc, "even the peanut who collects the tickets."

"By working at it, kid," the collector said, "by industrious application to contemplation and study, you, too, may come to occupy this sacred spot and enjoy a prospect of the same exacting magnitude."

"Am I hearing you or an automatic recording passing by?"

"I'm glad you've asked the question, for it presents an issue eminently referable to the Minister of Transport, who, as everyone knows, can answer anything in due passage of time."

"I've seen you before," Marc said.

"I rejoice in your great good fortune."

"The Playhouse," Marc said. "I knew you had to be a peanut. The repertory company. The school matinees. You were a spot of blood in *Macbeth*. And a toga in *Julius Caesar*."

"Certainly not," said the ticket collector, "neither blood nor toga. I was the royal doormat. Upon whom all wiped their feet. A modest coir doormat of Indian origin. Classically underplayed. As the role of the doormat must ever be. *Doormat steals the show*. Rave reviews. Yet in the years between, my brother, come these centuries of need, while here I stand at World's End awaiting Lord Olivier's confusion. No ticket. No explanation. And no escape except the royal doormat for me beneath his feet in his next production."

"Good luck to you, then," Marc said. "Breakfast at Tiffany's and dinner at Lazar's."

"May good fortune follow you also," said the ticket collector. "And after you, pursue your children and your children's children. One and all, may you live to great ages enriched by reams of little pieces of paper, ever of the colour required."

Thus Marc appeared to have gained a reprieve from the dungeon. And a better heart and humour, and a quickening stride carrying him in the direction of the bus.

The bus. Waiting in the rank. As it almost always was. Soon to be bound for all ports and points along the bay. Even the sun allowing itself a cautious celebration. Marc breaking into the obligatory run. Meaning, in turn, that the duffle bag of gear slung over his shoulder began banging into his back. Warm clothing in it. And clothing suitable for the warm. Packed this very morning in the fog. Marc knowing only too well the hot and cold flushes of spring. Wet suit. Jogging shoes. Electric razor. And the usual items with the usual sharp edges. All banging into his back like any other time.

No need to run for the bus. But if a fellow's got to run, he's got to run.

"I'm on the way, Gramps. Here I come. And half a day early. So I'm not squibbing it. How will it go for us? And for Gran?"

Marc boarding the bus, a foot on the step. A sudden stop, as before, as if caught by a pain.

Lucky the large woman with toes like chisels and heels like hammers wasn't still coming along behind.

TWO

----◆-◆-◆----

Leadbeater
Beating the Water

NOW FOR the learned Marcus Leadbeater. The Leadbeater most recently late. An account of relevant historical
facts.

Education as a way of life having passed from him onto
his successors.

"You know where you can keep it," he said, "and may
your portals never be darkened by my presence again."

Whereupon he departed from the halls of learning with
a blast of twin exhausts and a flurry of elegant chrome,
declining to return even for graduations. Which could have
lost him a pleasure or two of a non-academic kind.

Yet no one seriously expected him to seek or accept further employment. Perhaps he could have delivered the local
newspaper, but why deny others the pleasure?

Instead, he loafed about the house all day reading the
latest Bond. The latest *Journal of Defence Studies*. The
latest *Playboy*. The latest airmail edition of *The Times Literary Supplement*. Or—like the winding of a knowing old

clock—he'd charge himself up by way of preparation for whiling away the time at some other address.

"Applying tension to the mood," he'd say. "If you're not in the mood, you might as well sleep in the sun. Rain permitting."

Having generated the mood, Marcus Leadbeater might then decamp for one or another of his favourite haunts. Bushranger Bay. Oyster Beach; not infrequently in the summer when the girls might be seen in less than total attire. Indeed, at a distance, sometimes in none at all. Or he might head for some hideaway with a falsified name to put the spies off the track.

"I'm away," he'd call to Gran.

"I wish you'd tell me where."

"I'll not know till I'm there. Mermaid's Parlour even, if the ducky little critter allows me through the door."

And that, in rough-and-ready terms, with the usual blast of twin exhausts and the flurry of elegant chrome, would take care of him for the day.

"An inappropriate and childish practice" was the view of Miss Fidelia Forsythe and her sister next door, "which amounts to contempt for those of us who spend our busy lives worrying about him, is it not so, Harriet? And fuels our doubts about the company he keeps. Where and what, as if we didn't know, might the Devil's Dive and Bouncing Bertha's Bathtub be?"

Nemesis Beach, for instance, in the Prohibited Area.

There the visiting head of a foreign government strode down the sands and into the surf and never was seen again. Many were the theories. Simple was the truth. The sea-serpent, said the learned Leadbeater.

But Gran said, "That ends it, Marcus. If it drowns Prince

Hubert, you're as good as dead. What gives you the idea you're stronger in the surf than he?"

The learned Leadbeater had another name.

Gramps.

Which meant he'd been around in 1967, when Prince Hubert strode into the sea. Even around in 1927, topping sixth grade at primary school over Willie Westland, who'd come first every other year and believed it to be the will of God.

"And," Gran yelled after Gramps when the occasion called for it, "keep off the rocks at Riptide! Last week another life lost. All these big heroes carried off in freak waves. What's wrong with fishing from the pier like the little boy you really are?"

Another time: "Why, for pity's sake, must you go this morning anyway?"

A reasonable question.

"Are you hearing me? I sometimes wonder. I could be talking to a deaf man. Nemesis I absolutely forbid. Look what you've done to me, Marcus. Turned me into a nagging old shrew. I was a pretty young girl across whose lips there'd never passed a foul word until I met you."

There might have been a blast from the twin exhausts. There might have been the flurry of elegant chrome. Yet the vehicle might not have moved from where it gathered spiderwebs and grime.

As Miss Fidelia and Miss Harriet next door would tell anyone at the time, Gran spoke to people who weren't there.

Before Gramps retired (with the much-reported thankful sigh recorded for TV) he was dean of mathematics at that well-known university, occasionally handling a difficult problem for the Department of Defence. Which was why he had the open permit to enter the Prohibited Area. Leadbeater's slice of corruptsy.

"The permit, gentlemen, or I decline to add up your beastly sums! Then where will you be?"

By which ruse the learned Leadbeater was able to enjoy the spiritual luxuries of Nemesis that remained inaccessible to the rank and file. And thus aroused the hostility of students of "radical" mind who called him a Fascist and set his wastepaper basket alight and locked him in his office, not in serious expectation that he might burn to death. He leapt two storeys into the rosebed and the Fire Brigade came.

Before Gramps was a professor of mathematics he was navigator of a Pathfinder aircraft in the terrible war fought against Fascism, a mustering and posting which irked him at the time, for he'd counted on becoming a famous fighter pilot. (*"No hope, dear boy, of cramming you into the cockpit, at two hundred and two centimetres tall."*) But he was awarded the Distinguished Service Order, which more than assured his status with the girls.

Before that he was a schoolboy.

At first a notably grubby one, but around Year Nine became the self-elected victim of an abrasive campaign to clean up his public image.

Washing vigorously, often, from head to foot with Lifeline toilet soap to suppress the insidious body odours that were said to ruin reputations in hot classrooms. (The aromas of the body thus deferring to the reek of disinfectant.)

Slicking down his hair with Crawleigh's Brilliantine. (A gross hint of oil of roses.)

Minutely inspecting the mirror image of his teeth with

the aid of a magnifying glass and brushing until his gums bruised. (Gusts of Dobb's Dentifrice and Spearmint Chewing Gum.)

Forever changing his shirt and shining his shoes. (Residual smells of Cherub Laundry Soap, Red Star Starch, and Kookaburra Boot Polish.)

Thus night and day engaged in the endless quest to arouse the awed enthusiasm of girls who, like nine out of ten film stars, smelt largely of Flux. With the added dimension, direct from Paris by sea, of Metreman's Old French Lavender cologne, by courtesy of Mum's dressing table, usually in the absence of Mum.

The collective atmosphere of the average classroom or railway carriage before or after school thus generating a quality never taken into account by the Creator in his original calculations. Which, to a degree, prepared heaven for the basic aroma of generations to follow.

At about age fifteen, Year Ten, the tongue of Gramps started obeying his brain instead of flushing his cheeks with humiliation. An exciting talent leapt to his command, as if bestowed by a benevolent but mischievous spirit.

Leadbeater had acquired wit!

With polish and humour and ease he could tease the increasing number of girls who stimulated his romantic inclinations. And the better his mood, the more eloquent his tease, and the more widely his inclinations roamed. Gorgeous Gertie and Dazzling Doris and Scintillating Cynthia and many in between. To say nothing of Bashful Bunny encountered long afterwards and in the end answering to the call of Gran.

Leadbeater's line was a brand of double-talk delivered with a straight face, as instructed by Papa, the holy father, who wore a tall mitred cap and classic robes of cream and gold when he entered the cathedral in procession on Sundays.

"There are critical commandments not counted among the ten, my son," Papa announced to Gramps at a fairly early age.

"The Eleventh Commandment, of which I at present speak, was given in confidence to Moses by the Angel of the Lord and has been passed down by word of mouth to the chosen few, as now I pass it down to you. The Twelfth Commandment, a confidential matter, is for another time. Ask me again when you're forty-nine."

So Papa assumed the manner and words of the Angel as addressed to Moses. No smile upon the Angel's face: none upon Papa's. No twinkle in the Angel's eye: Papa just as grave. *"The Eleventh Commandment urges thus: Thou shalt not laugh at thine own joke: he who thus obliges God shall be favoured by God."*

Of this, Gramps remained mindful, even when he was so funny he was close to death from the pain of it. Even when his victims, who knew nothing of the commandment, turned angry or confused or violent or suicidal.

The older Gramps grew and the more he loved people, the more he teased the people he loved, and the more were they whose friendship he never regained. The tease being irrepressible and the word mightier than discretion and the regrets never foreseen, only grieved over afterwards.

"But," Gramps said to Marc, "I've never sharpened my wit on the sea-serpent. It's not worth the candle. If she has a fault, boy, it's her direct line of approach. As subtle as a king wave. One gulp and like Jonah you're gone. I never utter a word out of place in her hearing. Just touches me forelock, and heads for home as fast as I can beat the water."

Statements of the kind eventually began to bore the rising generation.

"Fair go," Marc said. Five months past. Last Easter Sunday. In a mood as unsubtle as the sea-serpent. "You know I can't believe that rubbish anymore. I'm a hundred and ninety centimetres tall."

Outside the moving bus there loomed an emptiness of sea, sky, and glare.

"You should have bitten your tongue that day," the glare said. "Look where it led."

Misplaced midwinter all around on that day. A shrieking atmosphere laden with salt five hundred metres inland. Weather meant for the seals and the penguins setting in at a season and in a place where it had no business to be.

The only time out-of-doors spent rushing for another log of firewood or sprinting from the car to the fish-and-chips shop for a change of diet.

"Take a look at my chin," Marc said on that day, over the chess board. "That's not pimples, mate. That's a shaving rash. Induced by the rough edge of the razor you gave me. Would you have me humouring you in your old age? I'm reading books now with words of three syllables. I've even read the title page of *War and Peace*."

"The comic-book edition," Gramps said. "So what'll you be saying to the unsuspecting sea-serpent when next she rears her head?"

"I'll be telling her to get lost."

"I sorrow for thee," Gramps said, "though I sorrow more for me."

"No, Gramps. Don't take it that way. Not even as a joke."

"What joke?"

"You know. The straight face. The Eleventh Commandment."

"So at my age I'm supposed to start shrugging off your deadly misuse of language?"

"Gramps, no."

"My overlong association with the human tragedy termed the education system warns me that lingual finesse amongst the barbarians must ever be a hope for the future. Along with interstellar travel. Before you exercise the thrust of your wit, make sure you can get along without the target of your wit. Do you want to scare me off?"

A kid needed to be the grandson of a mathematician and the great-grandson of a bishop to take it without bursting into tears.

Despite the weather, next morning Gramps was saying, "We need air, you and me. Have we ever had a difference before, a serious one? Let's go find the sea-serpent. Let's settle it."

They settled it.

Yes, sir.

Like Gramps (Marcus Leadbeater XV), and the holy father of Gramps (Marcus Leadbeater XIV), Marc, too, had his other name: Marcus Leadbeater XVI. Or Sixtieth. Or Six Hundredth. (No one, no one could say.)

This interesting concurrence of Marcus Leadbeaters ended but rarely in confusion, for Grandpapa, aged a hundred and three, lived upon a mountain a great distance off, in declining health, having been in the grip of a highly disturbed digestive system for forty-seven years.

And the lovely Gramps. No chance of his ever being mistaken for another. As tall as an open doorway, some said, and as rugged, in what once was called his long and lingering prime.

As for Marc. Not likely to make the physical might, mass, or height of Gramps. Missing out by the thickness of a single volume of the Compact Edition of the Oxford English Dictionary. And unlikely to achieve distinction in higher mathematics, having achieved none in vulgar fractions. And never likely to make a respected name in the Church, preferring almost anything to public devotions. The suspicion being, in the family, that he might at some distant date acquire a reputation by acting out a few fragments from the lives of others before the cameras or the footlights.

Now, seated upright in his bus, fidgeting, wishing for the bus to take wings. To be there and back. To have come and gone.

———◆◆———

THREE

Leadbeater:
Up to Date

LEADBEATERS IN general: a summary. For all persons
in some respect summarize those who went before.

Captain Marcus Leadbeater, a modest man, distinguish-
ing himself with the Federal forces at Fishers Hill, Virginia,
on September 22, 1864; within the week, in the chaplain's
tent, joining in wedded bliss with the general's daughter—
who had no business in Virginia except her spirited love
for Leadbeater.

Sergeant Marcus Leadbeater, Royal Marines, a brash
and boastful fellow, arriving with the First Fleet at Botany
Bay, New South Wales, on January 26, 1788. Much com-
promised in the course of the long voyage. Incurring the
displeasure of his commander, who commanded, "Marry
them. Starting with Mabel."

Marcus Leadbeater, a pious man, his wife, Charity (née
Beckett), and children Matthew, Marcia, Luke, and John,
landing at Boston, Massachusetts, among a stalwart company of Puritans on April 14, 1632, immediately establish-

ing a uniquely exclusive school for the religious and social advancement of maturing young ladies.

Marcus Leadbeater, Esquyer for the body of our Sovereign Lord the King, an ambitious young gentleman, taking to wife Amabel, eldest daughter of Sir Morgan Ieuan, on November 23, 1489, shortly thereafter warmly supporting Amabel's wish that her younger sisters in Cardiff be allowed to visit at Court, one by one, from time to time.

Records surviving from the Middle Ages bear witness to Marcus Leadbeater, a reckless upstart, beheaded at Westminster for treason, July 16, 1208, twenty-nine maidens, of a kind, clamouring in vain at the gates for stay of execution.

And many, no doubt, were they, among Leadbeater males, who gained no fame, no infamy, and no particular note, except modesty, brashness, boastfulness, piety, ambition, recklessness, and enduring commitment to the shapely maid and the pretty face. As for the Marcia Leadbeaters, appearing and reappearing through several hundred years of documentation, little may be relevant to this tale other than the very few who regarded the amatory adventures of their brothers with patience, good humour, or approval.

To this general statement one must add a further Marcus Leadbeater, born Greenwich, England, 1779, of whom Marcus, born Melbourne, Australia, a couple of centuries later, gave indications in boyhood of close kinship.

These two Leadbeaters, Gramps said, stood apart, but side by side in the annals of the family.

The shy, gangling, accident-prone Leadbeater (born 1779) giving but few early indications of developing in adult life into the remarkable human being who strode supreme across the classic European stage.

Leadbeater was the Prince Charming. He came. He conquered.

Many said, "Who needs Nelson? Who needs Wellington? Send Leadbeater to Paris for St. Crispin's Day."

Henley-on-Thames. 1812. Friday. The thirteenth. The river running strongly, running deep. Leadbeater, aged thirty-three, in part effecting a splendid death. A special human being placing the value of the life of his tabby cat alongside his own.

Uncounted cultured ladies of London, Copenhagen, Berlin, and St. Petersburg gave every appearance of mortal grief. And fifteen thousand women, at one count, wept as the funeral cortege passed through the London streets.

Which finds Marc stepping down from the railway bus at the end of his journey. A favoured small town named for an ancient resort far away beside an ancient sea.

This small town receiving Marc at its edge hours earlier than announced; a prospect appealing to a heroic streak last evening.

"Three-thirty," he'd said to Gran. Into the telephone. But meaning ten-thirty. Hoping the surprise would take the pressure off. A hope that looked foolish now.

When you get there and you're face to face, what do you say?

Thus Marc addressed himself.

Do you flash the famous family grin? Do you wear the downcast look? Or turn the key waiting in the lock and burst in?

Marc, at the kerb, at the edge of town, shaking his head.

"To be early is a humane response to a complex situation."

That had been Mum's formal reaction. As if addressing herself to an examination question. A not uncommon approach of hers. Well, all those years; teaching notes in one hand, chalk in the other . . .

"I like your reasoning," she'd then said, as if correcting the question and pencilling her comments in the margin.

Well, Marc had liked it, too. But under the hard light of day, he'd have been better off waiting at home.

Did Gran need him early?

Did Gran need him late?

Better to have chained himself to the bedpost. Or accepted the challenge of entertaining himself elsewhere. By dying of nerves. Or by dying of not being humane. Or by dying of reproach. Or by dying of conscience.

End of term again.

A whole sixteen days for dying twitch by twitch of grief.

Well, he could've read a book or two; fortunately having just found Wodehouse. Could've played some tennis. Could've seen some shows. Could've taken Drama at the College of the Arts, if he'd thought of it. But when Gramps and Gran have been giving you the horrors for five months straight, what else is remembered?

Would've been better if Mum had said, "It's too soon to wade out into life. The undertow'll pull you down. You'll drown. As effectively, as finally, as your reckless old grandfather. Why don't we, just you and I, while we're still of an age to tolerate each other—putting your sisters out to grass—pack a bag and catch a flight to Tahiti? They owe me a flight. I'm confident we can wangle another for you."

In point of fact, she'd come up with the opposite.

Hearken unto Mum! Born an O'Reilly!

"When," said Mum, "we start thinking about supporting

others in their darkest hours, we act as conscience guides us, because conscience comes from deep wells of awareness given us when we were born."

There'd been Irish priests in the family a couple of generations back. As well as leprechauns.

"Be warned," said Mum, "do not confuse the signals from your conscience with the wish to make a good fellow of yourself."

She could have been reading from an idiot sheet in front of a camera for a religious programme.

"I don't know what you mean, Mum."

"I hope you never do. Except that I'm allowing you to go ahead with this idea because your father and I believe in you."

Nice yoke to dump about the neck of a kid. Like, it's all your doing, kid. Like, what you do with your life is your funeral, kid. Like, why don't you go hang yourself? You'll find the rope's in the toolshed on your way out.

"And while," said Mum, "you go on acting sensitively and responsibly, parents like us step aside. We reject the negative view that young people are bound to fail under pressure."

Like, if you do fail, kid, don't come whining to us.

Mum still reading from the idiot sheet.

Perhaps the programme was a round-table discussion for experts on raising children. Into which she'd stumbled by accident.

To which the noble kid delivered the manly response: "I reckon Gran can still do with all the support that's coming. Especially from me. I won't be letting you down, Mum. Or her. Or Gramps. You'll see."

A grown-up exchange of view. Like putting your signature, fearlessly, to your own death warrant.

"I must've been possessed."

But upon further reflection it sounded more like Mum simply serving the interests of the females of the house!

What do you bet they were planning a couple of weeks for living the natural female life? Leaving Dad, high and dry, as it were, forever on his way to London. And this here adolescent male property stranded a hundred kilometres from his personal funk hole. Far from high and dry. And about to be knocking on Gran's door. With everything awful lying in wait on the inside. Like Mademoiselle Guillotine.

One way only for the blade not to fall.

Are you hearing me up there, you people in charge of gravity!

Gran's got to do everything right, or all the happy times will be dragged through the muck. No angry questions from her. No bitter judgements. No saying, *You and that seaserpent.* No yelling, *Why didn't you stop him?* No screaming, *Whose side are you on, you grandson of the devil?*

Has that bus really gone? Can't we turn back the clock and come to the corner again? Can't I not get off? Can't I just go back home to my mum?

My mum should've said an arranged time is an arranged time. She should've said, What's wrong with half past three as planned? A nice social hour for tea and cakes. With bed not like a million years away? What's this crazy compulsion to pile agony on agony when you shouldn't go at all?

So she pecks me on the cheek and ruffles my hair. "Call me if there's a problem."

First thing wrong I've got to do me hair again and second thing wrong is me problem. Do you hear me calling, Mum?

Mum as silent as Service Difficulties and Faults. At her Foreign Aid Club drinking coffee. Beth and Jo Anne rifling my cupboards, feeling under my mattress, looking for sexy magazines that are none of their business. One of these days I'm going to turn on them, real savage.

Disaster as close as a good spit in a high wind and Mum doesn't give me a thought.

Up through town, round the bend, across the road, and Gran's door leaping up at me like a runaway truck.

That great slab of wood opening. Mademoiselle Guillotine poised to drop. Gran standing in the half-light. Eyes filling with tears. Hers and mine.

Oh, Gran, I forgot me umbrella. If you're not going to kill me, at least keep it dry.

You're ancient like the rocks and I'm a know-nothin' kid. Give a thought to it. The non-functional Leadbeater. Never had a girlfriend. Not even my delectable Rosemary. Except on stage. And for ten minutes in the pantry when I was fourteen. Never been in danger of gettin' caught. Never had a whippin' for being wicked. Poor bloomin' me. What do I do with weeping grandmothers?

"Oh, my beautiful boy," she'll sob.

Stone blind to pimples and the length of nose.

Then she'll sob some more. "You and my beautiful silly old man. What are we to do without him?"

At the very best, disaster setting in like fourteen days and fourteen nights of solid rain.

Happy holiday time, here we are again.

Marc, still at the edge of town, turning heavily on his heel, overlooking open sky and sea.

All calm down there across the bay.

There ought to be bloody waterspouts and shipwrecks and distress rockets. There ought to be people screaming,

"Save me. Save me." There ought to be naval battles and lifeboats and rescue helicopters and TV newsmen.

But what have we got? Iridescent blues like a colour chart for somebody's bathroom. And a haze. Pretty as a picture. The sort you see in art shows under clear plastic sheets on rainy days in the park. All iridescent, and streaky, and pale.

"Streaky?"

The pained question arriving express from deep space.

"Streaky like bacon? Is that what you're saying? And pale? Like some spook with a hangover? Like after a heavy night out on the Milky Way? Is that the best you can do?"

Marc sighing. "You must know how it is. Why are you so hard on me?"

"A rugged character's not asked to turn soft just to mark his appointment to the committee ruling an emerging world inhabited by amoebas. Take it from me, kid, in their company, even you're beautiful."

"You should be sleeping in your grave, old man, nice and quiet and civilized."

Hollow laughter faint among the stars.

Marc sighing. "Well then, sleeping like it's for getting your strength back. For coming up out of the sea as if you'd been gone only a minute. Then I wouldn't be in this fix. Still bleeding my heart out every day. Why don't you give it a try?"

No answer from Gramps.

Marc looking back to town. Back to Gran in her darkened house. Her house smelling of books in need of a dust and Chinese rugs in need of a clean and everything in need of sunlight.

So what about the sunlight of this here kid walking in bright and early?

That's what you're here for, kid. Grit your teeth. Start shining.

Marc hitching up his duffle bag. Heartbeat knocking the wind out of him.

Street full of parked cars. Kids in all kinds of gear. Kids looking real freaky, real great. The end-of-term look. Everyone preparing for it since midwinter. Same as Marc. But different.

Kids down from the city over the weekend wearing the parentally controlled look. The back-to-the-family-beach-house look. "We've been coming here since we were two!" Kids wearing the bored look that would have gone for someplace hot enough to support a suntan.

"I know what you mean," Marc said to Marc.

Gramps hurtling back from deep space.

"The expectations of your spoilt-rotten generation! Next it'll be the moon for Easter and Mars for Christmas. When I was your age, the thought of stepping along this street . . . Bay lapping at one end. Ocean raging at the other. Same bay. Same ocean. Any time of year. Copping an eyeful of the beautiful girls. What's changed? Not the street or the bay or the ocean or the girls. What do you mean bored?"

"It's in the viewpoint, Gramps. We were wearing nappies with big safety pins. Then little short pants with big buttons. We used to think grownups were gods."

"I don't like the trend, boy. Who's perfect? Are you telling me you are?"

But Gramps hadn't often been the one to cut the young ones down. Except the once.

When those grown-up kids called him Fascist and came within moments of burning him to death, he dragged himself out of the thorns in the rosebed and went through them with his fists.

"Morons. Misfits. Go cauterize your clichés. Go sterilize your stupidities."

When the police came, he said, "It's an internal matter. Don't bug me and don't bug them."

Marc plodding through the town, duffle bag lurching into his back. "I'm sorry, Gramps, for everything about the last day."

Not a word from the old spook.

Hundreds of times walking with him through this town. Never giving a thought to anything but the completeness of the moment. Never considering that days with Gramps were not destined to go on forever.

Marc catching the eye of a girl. Her glance and his glance meeting for an instant; lost in the instant; nothing left but a bruise somewhere.

Marc knowing as quick as the moment that Gramps would have given her the eye. Given her the twinkle. Let her know that here was an old bloke who knew what it was like inside.

Hello there. Hello, girl. Hi.

And she might have got the message. Or might have been turned away. Or might have thought, Fifty years, old man. Fifty years too late for one of us and fifty years too soon for the other. Hi.

The meeting of Marc and the girl who passed by.

Gramps, Marc said, bring her back for me, please.

Silence from the Milky Way.

Marc flopping onto a green seat of iron bolted to the

pavement so that kids with nothing better to do couldn't take it apart or take it away or heave it over the nearest cliff.

The girl with the eyes that were blue or hazel or green. With the hair that was dark or fair. With the nose that was turned up or straight. With the lips that parted for an instant, or made no recognition.

He couldn't tell. He couldn't remember.

Like a moment she had come and gone. Gone like Gramps, for good and all.

FOUR

➤◆◆➤

The Mysterious World of M. Leadbeater

MARC COMING to a stop in the middle of a stride in the middle of the street. As if shot.

The gate lying open to the house of Gramps and Gran just across the way.

Marc stopping several paces short of it, the wound striking him to the heart.

He forgot it was a busy street. Forgot that humans on foot hadn't been a match for wheels in thousands of years.

Hudd and Sons.

What had they to do with this?

"Never knew them without a shop full of dreams for sale," Gramps used to say. "Broken dreams. Ended dreams. Though they can't die for each and all. Any more than I. Any more than you."

The shocking hoarding in red, yellow, and black obliterating the world:

OUTSTANDING EDWARDIAN RESTORATION

ON LARGE GARDEN SITE

Ten distinctive rooms with every desired convenience.
To be sold complete with numerous fittings & furnishings.
Suit academic, professional, or company.
Immediate vacant possession to cash buyer.
Inspection strictly by appointment.
AUCTION HERE, 11 A.M., TUESDAY, SEPTEMBER 22
HUDD AND SONS
Licensed Real Estate Agents and Auctioneers
ALWAYS SERVING YOU

Inside Marc, a wasteland, in which a distant voice, his own, was struggling to make itself heard: Gran, how can you do this terrible thing?

Sell all the things he's made?

Fittings, they call them. Are diamonds common stones?

Room by room making them over. Every one the work of his own hands. Half the pictures. Half the stained glass. All the panels.

The happy-ever-afters in my good dreams. In my bad dreams something had happened to this house and I'd be looking for it. And getting desperate. And more desperate. And I'd wake up sick.

But then I'd know that it'd still be waiting for me, even though Gramps wasn't anymore.

September 22. Tuesday. Tomorrow.

It's like you never cared, Gran. Like you're putting what's left out of reach of me. It's like he never counted. Or I never counted.

I thought I was the special kid who came. Who used to plead with you: "I don't really have to go home. Please, Gran. Mum and Dad would hardly notice. They'd never miss me at school. All those thousands of kids driving everyone crazy. How could they miss me? Gran, it might be a year before I'm back. It might be never. Get on the phone. Tell 'em I've got something catching."

Looks different now.

Looks like I was never more than the kid who went back to town.

How can the garden that Gramps grew be sold? Gramps getting weeded out of it like the thistles.

The things he made grow in this dry old sand. Teasing them if he reckoned they were slow. Like he teased horses and dogs and cats and the pigeons on the roof. Treating them all like people. Teasing them just the same. I was in it with him, Gran. Believing in what we did together. Even when he was teasing. You must've been in it when I wasn't there. Or was he left on his own?

Did he end up thinking, I've had enough of being alone when Marc goes back to town? And sank, because time had come and I'd mocked him and the waves were there.

I hear my dad saying, No one can empty himself out forever like Gramps. Dad saying, If you've got pests in the garden you get yourself some sprays. Gramps doing it the hard way. Charming the snails back into their shells. Charming little boys, like I used to be, with clumsy hands and heavy feet, right out of their minds.

How come, Gran, he didn't charm you?

As for the green things and growing things. Everything growing like mad night and day. Everything responding. Even when his jokes were dead awful. Cutting those lawns every week when every other lawn around had browned off for the summer.

"Stupid lawns," he'd say. "All their brains are under-ground."

The trees getting bigger and bigger. Leaning against the walls. Drooping on the roof. Hardly able to hold themselves up. Forcing us to lop their tops off in the bushfire season.

"Sorry," he'd be saying, "but you've only got yourselves to blame. You're not mountain ash. You're not red cedars. All we expect of you is a little shade on hot days." Then we'd dress their wounds with disinfectant.

Even the seeds leaping up. Gramps having a quiet word with the slowcoaches: "You down there. Don't be cowed by the dazzling things they say on the pack. If you can't live up to your publicity, don't get in a sweat. Come on up and I'll give you special care."

Up they'd come.

When they say *furnishings* up for auction, they mean up for the guy with the fattest wallet. They mean that you and Hudd and Sons are on the same side.

When I was a little kid I reckoned we had sacred relics here that people fought wars over. Would you be selling him for a relic if we'd given you the chance?

First time I haven't felt awful about our not being able to find him. The one stroke of luck we had that day.

The wasteland. The winds of despair. Beyond which a woman's voice was telling him she'd been stuck on the road in her panting Corolla for longer than she considered wise.

"Is that properly the place to stand? All we need is some young guy screaming through here and he'll iron us flatter than his board."

A *scarred* Corolla, as well as panting.

Ashen, Marc could see only her smile and he raised an arm to the appalling pronouncement.

"Lady. It's where I come every time. But my Gramps is

dead. What's she doing, for God's sake? Does she have to
sell his house? And garden? And all the things he's made?
No one telling me. Not even my parents. Were they afraid?
Or ashamed? Selling it tomorrow and I arrive here today."

The woman said, "I'm Beatrice." But he didn't properly
see her. Or know her.

"When you need me, take the next corner on the right,
then the next on the left."

Was that supposed to mean something?

"Do me a favour, Marc Leadbeater. Get your body off
the road before we're killed. Number 226. Round the corner
on the right. Then the corner on the left. On the way to
the surf. The quintessential small white cottage called The
Little Jubilee. With drinks in the fridge and fruit cake in
the cupboard, if the resident predators haven't consumed
us before you get there. If a construction of bare bones
crawling with savage black ants answers the door, speak
up. Bare bones may be hard of hearing."

She was gone, several less patient vehicles pressing behind, and Marc, with a hand to his brow and fingers in
his hair, was edging past the monstrous hoarding and heading for the house along the path that Gramps had made
stone by stone. The house where Gramps had been king
for fourteen years. And Marc had been clown prince.

Marc stopping on that path.

How can she do this to me? If money's her language I'll
raise it myself, but how can she get round the law? And
how do you turn nothing into gold in twenty-four hours?

Twelve dollars on Saturdays cutting lawns for the East-
lakes. Fourteen if it's raining and the ground's like a sponge.
Always prayin' for rain. Fifteen dollars from Dad. Account
standing at $244.32 plus interest accrued.

You're weak in the brain, M. Leadbeater.

How much do houses cost down here at the end of the world? Forty thousand? Fifty thousand? How much do houses cost anywhere?

Dad on the London trip. No hope of catching him till London's wrapped up and gone. No hope, anyway.

I personally finance the social welfare budget, he says. Everyone thinks I'm an oil well. I fly for love, he says, and for the pleasure of subsidizing the federal government's grandiose schemes.

Which leaves me, thought Marc, to raise the money on my own. And I wish I could swear that not a stick of this house nor a stone of it will get away. But in twenty-four hours?

Marc reaching for the door knocker, the magic Garuda bird of once-glistening alloy brought by Gramps from Java, 1963. Tarnished now from years of exposure to sea air. But still the magic Garuda bird.

An arrested moment before the striker made contact. A temptation to tear it from the door and run.

"What do I say to her before I throw up?"

But the striker struck. And struck loudly the second time. And, as always, ending to Marc's ritual soft tap. The *Here I am. It's me.*

To which no one stirred. To which no one came.

Marc waiting, almost without breath, ear pressed to the door.

"Oh, come on," he said aloud. "I'm getting the twitch."

Not implying that Gran was away for a minute or two, or for an hour or two. Meaning that Gran had gone. Gone like the girl with the eyes. Gone like yesterday. Gone like Gramps. Gone like all the magic parts of life.

The unanswered door. Why?

His hand slipping from the magic Garuda bird.

I was speaking to her last night. I'll be with you at three-thirty, I said, and like we arranged, we'll go somewhere different every day. I'll show you everywhere we ever went. And where we went that last time. I'll do my best, Gran.

"*Very well, Marc,*" he heard her saying. "*Three-thirty you'll be here. And then somewhere different every day. As you promised.*"

And when I hung up I said to my mum, I'll be there by ten-thirty. So she won't be waiting round all day. And Mum reckoned that was being sensitive. And I haven't dreamt up what either of them had to say. But what was Gran getting at? *As I promised?* As if she hadn't been a party to it. But how can you be sure what really happened back in those terrible days?

Now Gran packing up overnight and clearing off before eleven in the morning? It'd take some doing. Or is she in there lying beside the telephone? All those silent rooms waiting for me to come breaking in?

Marc's ear still pressed to the door, straining for the slightest sound.

Nothing moving in there.

Stepping back, step upon step, until he was in the clear and able to see how the windows were shut and the blinds drawn.

Marc muttering, going off to the side, then down by the side. The garden everywhere looking limp and trafficked, though severely neat, everything feeling the strain of being held in readiness for inspection strictly by appointment. Something priceless having departed. The touch of Gramps having departed.

In the car shelter, the Jaguar (the twin exhausts, the elegant chrome), as if it hadn't moved since the day the army brought it home.

The Mark II. Year of manufacture, 1963. The only car, in Marc's memory, that Gramps ever owned. With the steel-grey duco and the renovated red leather. With the rebuilt rust areas and the renewed red carpet and the repolished walnut and the reconditioned classic straight six.

"Something to do with the ethos of one's own age," Gramps used to say. "I didn't fancy one when they were new. But anyone could afford them when I bought mine, if you weren't scared of building them up again.

"Listen to her purrrrrrr. That's style, boy. That's pedigree. That's my pussy cat."

Pressure down in one tyre.

All surfaces dulled by salt air and wind-driven spray and bird droppings. Even spiderwebs in the radiator grille.

Aloud! "It's like Gran hasn't been here for years. What the hell's going on?"

What was I speaking to on the phone last night? Some damn recording? Selling everything out from under me. Putting my Gramps on the market. Leaving his car to rot. Not even pumping up his tyre.

Marc striding across the patio through the maze of pots and tubs to the French doors. Dropping his duffle bag. Beating angrily against the glass.

Peering in. Curtains drawn.

"Why are you hiding in there?"

Beating with those fists.

"Open up!"

Beating and banging at the glass doors.

A voice intruding: "What are you up to over there? What are you doing at that house? You've no right there."

The voice of Miss Fidelia Forsythe. Which covered it.

The head and shoulders of Miss Fidelia having appeared above the side fence as if she were very tall. About two and a half metres. Arm raised. Mouth open. "Marc Leadbeater? Is it you I'm seeing? What are you making all that noise for?"

His temper burst through the top. "Minding my own business, lady. What's left of it."

"That'll do now. We don't expect that kind of talk from you."

Marc clenching his fists. "Try to understand. Please. I'm trying to get my Gran to open up and she won't."

"Of course she won't. She lives somewhere else. As you know."

"As I do *not* know! She didn't tell me. My mum didn't. My dad didn't. No one's breathed a word of it before I heard it from you just now."

"Of course they told you. You're hysterical. Isn't he, Harriet? Harriet and I think it would be expedient and proper for you to control yourself. In a properly masculine manner becoming the grandson and namesake of Professor Marcus Leadbeater of highly respected memory."

"I'm not hysterical. They didn't tell me. And that's not proper either. I've come down here to stay like I always do and no one answers the door."

"My poor boy. It really is clear that you're out of touch with reality. Isn't that so, Harriet? Out of touch. Very sad. One mourns for the Leadbeaters. They are not as they were."

I can't cope with this lady.

"*The pair of them,*" Gramps used to say, "*patrolling the fence top like a couple of demented magpies.*"

"Okay, lady. You'd know. I'm bananas. I'm hysterical. I'm the magpie. We're all nuts."

"Rudeness," Miss Fidelia said sternly, "doesn't enhance your grandfather's memory. Temper won't either. You'll put your hand through the glass and get a nasty injury. That's Harriet's opinion. And mine."

Marc squeezed his eyes shut. "Lovely lady. Please. Where do I find my Gran?"

"Mrs. Leadbeater has not considered it necessary to take us into her confidence. Nor have we been able to ascertain her present address through any other channel."

Miss Harriet, having just acquired exceptional height also, or the upper rung of a second stepladder, wobbled into view.

Miss Fidelia went on: "She left here in a taxicab on the fourth of August. Carrying suitcases. Three suitcases. One, the leather portmanteau used by Professor Leadbeater during his last lecture tour of the United Kingdom. And five plastic bags. The blue teapot. The Wedgwood jug. The latter, absurdly, full of milk. We haven't seen her since. Hudd's sign went up the same day."

"I'm not dead sure who's the nut round here," Marc said. "I've been speaking to her on the phone."

"Then," said Miss Fidelia, "you must give us her number so that Harriet and I may speak to her also. There are matters about which the Hudds, dreadful people, will not advise us. Which isn't good enough. Are we casual acquaintances? Are we beneath consideration? Fourteen years. Side by side. Neighbours, Forsythes and Leadbeaters together through fair weather and foul. Through flood and fire. Ever ready to lend a hand. Ever alert to the slightest need. Hasn't it been so, Harriet?"

Inside Marc a strong voice issuing a warning: *They're up to their old tricks.*

So he slung his duffle bag over his shoulder, sharp objects spiking his back, and shouted, "There's nothing I can tell you. There's nothing I know. There's nothing for me here. I'm going to go."

Oh *no*, he thought. The family will kill me if I grow up to be a poet.

He headed off across the patio in the opposite direction, ignoring Miss Fidelia. For she called, the voice following him, as he ran round the far side, back to the open gateway, back to the street, back into town.

Running all the way.

Back to the same iron seat, painted green, bolted to the pavement.

There he flopped at one extreme end. At the other extreme end a snappy terrier tugged against a short tether.

"Shut up," Marc said.

Then addressed himself silently, chest heaving, nerves all over the place: I must've been out of my little mind setting foot in this town again. What's gone is gone . . . A whole three months waiting for it, sweating on it. I should've made it three years *at least.*

"Shut up," he said to the terrier.

I'm a mental incompetent. The clock's invincible. You can't reverse it.

"Oh, shut up, dog!"

Those terrible old magpies. How did he stand them all those years? Sharpening their claws on his fence. Poking their beaks through the cracks. I can't understand why they're so good-looking. They ought to have horns under their hats.

Subsiding into a daze. Though it might have been a fever. Not even seeing the beautiful girls passing by. Giving him the eye. Never seeing them, really, anyway.

Sighing also. As if suddenly aged.

I don't see the point of hanging round. I'm a superfluity. And if I try living here in the middle of the main street, they'll run me in as a vagrant.

What's my Gran mean by answering the phone when she doesn't live here? The only choice she gives me is to catch the next bus out.

"Oh, shut up, dog! Do you know what you are? You're the reason why I go for pussy cats!"

Across the road, a short distance, a shopfront started spelling out words through the fogs and bogs and noises in his head.

HUDD AND SONS

SINCE 1892

ALWAYS SERVING YOU

Marc read it several times.

"Hilarious," he said. "Hear my raucous laughter."

Which prompted him to haul on his duffle bag and add a few thoughts: If you don't mean it, you've only got yourselves to blame. It's a dangerous world you live in, Mr. Hudd and Sons. Time to start serving me.

"As for you, you little tripehound, count yourself lucky I'm not allowed to kick dogs, or you wouldn't have a working rib left in your body."

FIVE

A Leadbeater for Dreadful Emergencies

A SHOP full of dreams, as Gramps used to say. Dreams on offer. Dreams for sale. Make your selection and take it away . . .

In the side window, adjacent to the door, a small display. With *specials*.

Like supermarket soap?

$99,500. A house in the scrub.

$79,500. Something looking like a shed to put your bike in.

$59,500. Land. Bay view. Well, if you built a high house and raised a periscope from the chimney top.

$159,500. A house once visited by Marc on a rainy day. They had saucepans out to catch the leaks.

$249,500. For something that couldn't stand beside the house of Gramps and Gran.

"Oh, come on. A quarter of a million dollars for that!"

Something inside Marc was getting ready to break.

Leaning on the door to push it open against a hissing

device put there to keep it closed against flies, pests, and Leadbeaters.

Or, to effect the comprehensive capture of victims.

Each victim trapped by the crash of iron gates. And the shooting home of bolts. To the accompaniment of laughter written on the musical scale like dollar notes.

Marc in, the victim, breathless, flushed, anxious, assaulted by surprise.

A scene smelling strongly of newly laid claret-coloured carpet. And of newly sawn cedar and newly applied paint. And of something possibly wicked. Like after dark, when the little kids are asleep. A perfume with a component of musk.

The scene presided over by an ornamented young lady at the only desk in view. A desk, at a guess, acquired from the office division of the Swedish shop a hundred kilometres up the road.

This couldn't be the famous Hudd and Sons.

"Yes?" said the young lady.

A question delivered in a slow contralto that signalled: "Is real estate business really for you?"

Marc went on pulling himself together. For he'd half expected to meet Hudd in person. Partly mummified. Seated in the heart of an assembly of close relations in bowler hats, bow ties, starched wing collars, stovepipe pants, blindingly polished black boots, and a generally fusty smell.

Hudd, with an assembly of several white-haired sons almost as ancient as he, a number of grey-haired grandsons, and, like bulls at a tea party, two aggressive black-haired great-grandsons with super-tuned, turbo-assisted V8's ticking over in the company parking lot outside.

Hudd with the clan as a whole, in rows, as if posed for the ultimate family portrait: an illustrated supplement to a lesser genealogy of the Old Testament.

But Hudd was not to be seen!

Only this young lady again producing the tone that signalled questions.

"Yes?"

This upright, brightly painted young lady of about the same impact as Miss Gorgeous. The phenomenal Miss Georgina Griffiths. Responsible for an increasingly critical area of Marc's education. A crisis due only in part to Marc's impatience with the strictures of conventional grammar.

Marc, by association, caught up in a fantasy problem. Yet convinced that the façade presented by the young lady at the desk would be the outcome of high-level responses to detailed attention. Bringing to mind Captain Robert Leadbeater and the instrument dials of his 747, say, in a screaming cumulonimbus thundercloud over Southeast Asia.

Plucked eyebrows upon the young lady arching as if expressing continuing amazement; Marc for the moment aghast at the idea of the tweaking of each little plucking.

Disturbing tan; Australian winter being but twenty-one days gone. The method of acquiring the tan raising interesting projections.

Lips like Cupid's bow. Rendered in silvered purple.

Hair like a mop in electric shock. The creation of a mildly insane hairdresser?

The contours of her soft silk blouse Marc modestly choosing to avoid, dropping his eyes to the grubbied toecaps of his sneakers. And mightily clearing his throat: "I'm Marcus Leadbeater."

"Come to haunt us, I suppose?"

The young lady thus further catching Marc by surprise.

Well, she resembled more a way-out model in some TV commercial than an educated wit. So, acting upon the advice of his sainted grandfather, Marc took a breather before croaking, "I'd confirm that that's a fair statement."

Surprise now registering upon the face of the young lady. A phenomenon observed by Marc during quick but shy upward glances.

"Which Marcus Leadbeater?" he heard her ask. "Am I to shuffle the pack and pick the lucky card? Or has the joker picked me?"

Marc went on working at the frog in his throat. Though not entirely the classic lout, he had not yet attained the poise of El Suavo either.

Inwardly, he said, In my lifetime there have been but Leadbeaters three. My grandfather, who died in the sea. My great-grandfather, aged a hundred and three. And the joker, as you've rightly determined, who's me.

Outwardly, none of this was heard, because none of it would come.

"If you're here to stay," she said, "why not make yourself comfortable. What's wrong with the chair at your right?"

Then, as part of this week's free offer, she passed him a ticket.

For a complimentary ride on the ferry perhaps? To make up, belatedly, for the disastrously rough crossing of the Rip on his tenth birthday. A passage for twenty-three persons booked at the Courtesy Counter of Hudd and Sons!

What a day it had been.

"My card," she explained.

Marc read it at a glance:

HUDD AND SONS
SINCE 1892   ALWAYS SERVING YOU
Your representative: KAREN HUDD

So everything about the present day went on adding to
his astonishment.

This elegant creature was Hudd and Sons!

And not a day older than Miss Gorgeous. And dressing
with the same disregard for the lively imaginings of the
adolescent male.

"How much money," he gulped, "do you want for the
house?"

"Oh? Are we discussing a house? Which house?"

"What other house is there?"

Marc, having found voice, rushing on. "The house she's
got up for sale. The one she doesn't bother to live in. The
one with the fittings and furnishings and the distinctive
rooms and all the precious things she should've lodged with
the bank. And the immediate possession for the big cash
buyer. He'd better not turn it into a commune! I've been
round there banging on the door. I might as well have been
banging on the Sphinx."

"Do take a chair, Marcus Leadbeater. You're wearing
yourself out."

Marc expelling a large breath. "My interviews, lady, like
with the police constable, and the principal, and Miss Gorgeous, and you, I conduct standing up. I don't want to be
comfortable. I like wearing myself out. You're selling it
tomorrow. How much?"

"How much what?"

"Oh, lady! How much money? What else? Cornflakes?"

"I'm not in the back office, Marcus Leadbeater. Or stone deaf. Or more than usually insensitive."

Marc glaring at his sneakers. "From here the scenery looks different."

Hudd and Sons continuing in a pained contralto: "A question. Why are you here?"

"I've told you. To buy the house."

"I don't mean that. Because that's an absurdity. What can you accomplish by being here? I need to know. You're troubling me. You're throwing spanners in my works. Please don't avoid the question."

"I've answered your question!"

The shoulders of the young lady rising and falling. "There's no place for you here. I could do without it. I really could."

"So could I."

"Have you any idea of the kind of money you're talking about?"

Hudd and Sons curling a long finger with a luminous green nail about the end of her nose. Mark risking the quick and sneaky look. Thousands would have left home for it. Like Helen of Troy.

"Who can say how much it's going to bring? What the market returns. What the auction excites."

"Excites?"

"Whether they start jumping or go to sleep!"

"Am I hearing you say this auction's going to be a pop concert?"

"You're certainly not."

"But I'm hearing you say you don't know for how much!"

"Agreed."

"Lady, I'd go real big for some of this service your card reckons you've been handing out since 1892."

"Only since last March in my case."

"Are you selling this house or fooling around?"

"Committed to it, Marcus. And when we're talking price, the sky's the limit."

"The only limit I'm talking is the lowest. How much?"

Hudd and Sons lifting her eyes to the recently renovated ceiling. Panels of artfully compressed straw. "Why are you doing this? Are you the Marcus Leadbeater they keep in the back room? The one they bring out in dreadful emergencies? Do you seriously consider you should be here without your keeper?"

Marc glaring at his sneakers.

She said, "Why concern yourself with the lowest price? What's wrong with the highest?"

"You've got it by the tail, lady. I'm not paying the highest price for something that's mine."

Hudd and Sons leaning back in her swivel chair and aiming a short sharp breath at her left arched eyebrow. "Am I to take it that this is a serious discussion?"

"I've been telling you that."

"I see no need of it, and no reason for it. I'm amazed."

"That's because you're not me. What's the lowest price?"

"The reserve. As always."

"As always what?"

"No one," said Hudd and Sons, "can buy a house at auction for less than the reserve. You're not a child. If the reserve isn't reached, the house isn't sold. Unless the parties come to a private arrangement."

"Now we're talking turkey."

"Turkeys are not up for discussion. The auction must

fail before the reserve can be made public and turkeys can be introduced—if that's the way people feel. Until that occurs, the reserve's a secret between your grandmother and me. Otherwise why bother to hold an auction?"

"A good point. You still haven't told me how much."

"Have you heard anything? The price belongs to the day. To the conditions of the day. The conditions depend upon how many want the house. In this case, a great number. And how badly they want it. Even upon the weather. Whether the weather's a come-on and or a keep-away. If you're buying, you hope there's a blizzard or an outbreak of plague and no one else turns up. If you're selling, you hope the day is idyllic and they're fighting to get in the gate, as I believe they will be."

Marc daring to look her in the eye. A breath-catching eye emphasized with a black pencil line. "It's a wonder my Gramps doesn't come walking up out of the sea."

Her other eye was the same.

"His house getting sold off like a Sunday-morning market. No price except somebody's guess. One more time, lady. How much filthy lucre?"

"You've not inherited the family brain."

"You wouldn't know what I've inherited."

Both breath-catching eyes closing briefly. "I'm asking you to accept my well-meant invitation to sit. Whether you think better perpendicular or horizontal or strapped by your ankles to the chandelier. Whether you usually address the principal or the police constable or the fascinating Miss Gorgeous from the top of a tower or the bottom of a pit. Sit. I don't like your looming over me."

"I'm loomin', lady."

"Oh, dear Marcus . . . What's wrong with my lovely chair? Real leather. Real wood. Real bolts holding it together. All the bits assembled by me. All in the absence of my parents, who wouldn't recognize their precious office. If you tell me my chair isn't good enough and if these tastefully redesigned premises don't make you feel confident of my business imagination and integrity, I may hit you with a plate-glass window."

Marc went back to clearing his throat. And to glancing in the direction of her eyes again. Cautiously. The black pencil lines adding to the illusion that they were lit up.

He said, "I might answer better to Marc."

"I might answer better to Karen."

So he sidled onto her leather chair, edging it back and clasping at his knees.

"We've had an interest in common," she said with a breath that caused her shoulders to rise and fall. Everything else of interest rising and falling along with it.

Marc with a persistent frog in the throat.

She said, "Your grandfather. I often watched him go out of sight. He'd have been amused. I had no idea he was seventy-four."

Gramps strikes again, Marc thought. Why can't I get 'em excited? I won't be seventy-four for another hundred years.

Then she said, "Have you faced the problem of buying a house before? Have I faced the problem of auctioning a property such as this? My father in San Francisco for some Pan-Pacific powwow. Some powwow. He's been gone since May. And what's the date of the auction? To-morrow. Eleven a.m. My grandfather in Scotland for the Highland Games and I hear he's talking Trans-Siberian Railway . . ."

Marc's sneakers being out of view, he focussed on the crisp new map of the town survey lacquered to the wall.

Remarkable map. Crammed full of disturbing contours.

"You, Marc, have to accept that I have a right and a responsibility to conduct this sale according to the rules. If your problem conflicts with my responsibilities, I need to know what your problem is. I intend to see this sale completed successfully, to the satisfaction of all parties, without calling in help from outside."

Shades of Miss Gorgeous and her mind on nothing but practical matters. Like English grammatically structured. The mind of the male half of her class on nothing but the structure of her.

"Did you hear me, Marc?"

As Gramps once put it, Nature being what it is, beautiful girls in business make it damned near impossible for the healthy male to keep up with the facts in a crisis.

"Marc, have you an opinion?"

"Only about Gran and the house. Didn't she tell you?"

"Tell me what?"

"I thought everybody knew it was to come to me."

"That's not so, Marc. And never was. It's hers to live in or not to live in. To keep or not to keep. To do with as she pleases."

"He never meant her to sell it."

To his dismay his eyes filled with tears, and he shot up a hand, as if to claim, *I've got the floor. I haven't finished. Give me my say.*

"It's my Gran's house while she's alive. Everyone understands that."

Drawing the breath to make the words was a form of marathon up a long and steep hill.

"Then it comes to me. If I've turned twenty-five. Or I wait until I do. I might wait till I'm forty-five. But that's the understanding. And that's fine. I don't mind."

Marc again having to pause, tears shaming him, but with his hand still in the air asserting that the big part of him was meaning what it said.

"No one in the family's been arguing about it. I'm not as green as grass, lady. I'm not blind stupid. I know the family are keeping their arguments until later. When the arguments start, then I'll start worrying about 'em. But in the meantime, everyone knows what Gramps meant. And I know he meant me never to sell it, unless I share the proceeds dollar for dollar among a list of names as long as your arm. Nothing, Miss Hudd, is the way you're putting it."

"Have you finished?"

Marc dropping his hand.

"Let me tell you. Let me state. You must be aware that your grandfather hasn't left you a house. He's named you in a will that gives everything away twice, if not several times."

"No."

"Your family *and* the world have accepted it."

"The world's got nothing to do with it. You're twisting it to suit your own arrangements. To make yourself a fat commission to put you right with your parents while my inheritance goes down the drain."

Miss Hudd and Sons standing. "Do you know what you've just said?"

"Every word."

"Then retract it."

"Like hell."

She stepped around her desk and almost rushed at the door, there to drag it open against the pressure of the hissing device.

"Out! And I don't want to see you again unless accompanied by a responsible adult."

Marc feeling for his duffle bag and sensing against his leg the hard edge of the metal case of his razor. His vanity. His manhood. His gift from Gramps.

So Gramps said, "*Don't let your old mate down. Don't mess it up by being undignified.*"

Marc said, "I hear you, lady. You say you've been talking rights and responsibilities. So have I. No one told me the house was for sale. No one told me Gran isn't living here. I ring her on the telephone and she doesn't tell me she's not living here. I come down, as planned, as confirmed as recently as last night, to take her places where I'd been going with Gramps since I was three. Even to the place where he died. So I get here and find your sign, HUDD AND SONS. ALWAYS SERVING YOU. You tell me it's fair and square. I'm telling you it stinks."

Marc found himself on the pavement, where there was nothing to do but run.

SIX

Leadbeater at the Door

MARC FLOPPING on the yellow sands. Aching in body and head and heart. As if his world had lost all its happy destinations.

"As if there's nothing left to do about it and no one cares but me."

Even the last-minute good deed of turning up early turning into a weak-minded gesture.

His cheeks striking cold, but the rest of him prickling hot. A collision of temperatures like atmospheres in conflict. Like the classic storm.

"Stupid bloody will."

Hands falling into his lap as if unable anymore to bear the weight of air. Neck not able either to support the weight of care. Chin coming to rest almost on his chest. Breath arriving and departing in gusts. Morale related to a week of unbroken rain at the end of a month of unbroken cloud.

"That's a fair assessment, mate. Dead on target."

Marc in the wilderness of the post-Hudd and Sons

depression. Glooming on through badlands of anger and wastelands of misery.

"He's going to ruin my life with his stupid will. There should've been equal shares all around. I didn't ask for his house. Now it's going to cost me God knows what for the key of the door. It's obscene. Where do I get that kind of money? How do I ever pay it back?"

Marc heading off into the gloom and groans of the forests. Thinking of Leadbeaters down the ages. Miserable old spooks. Leadbeater invading Britain in 54 B.C. Leadbeater slaying the lion with the jawbone of an ass. Leadbeater and Eve in the Garden of Eden. All those guardian Leadbeaters withdrawing their favours, removing their protection, leaving one miserable kid to sink in his grandfather's soup.

"Especially, especially I don't like Gramps setting this up. How could he get it so wrong? How could he make such a mess of his sums? Giving everything away twice! And him supposed to be the mathematical saint."

Wastelands behind. Full of brambles. And disused mineshafts. And tiger snakes desperate for breakfast.

No turning back into that.

Wastelands ahead. Deserts. Skeletons of trees. Emaciated dinosaurs. Everything looking like Dali had painted it.

Nowhere out there you'd want to go either.

Wastelands in the middle. Bogs. Bottomless oblivion would be bliss. But what do you get if you're Marcus Leadbeater XVI? Not even boggy black oblivion closing mercifully over your battered head.

Marc raising his eyes as if weights were trying to keep them shut. Catching up on the change of scenery. Sea, sky, and a clamouring mob of fat seagulls crowding between the toes of his sneakers and the lapping edges of the bay.

"Oh, go away!"

This clamouring mob jostling and shoving and shouting from one to the other like a pack of 9 a.m. shoppers waiting for the doors to open on the clearance sale.

"Buzz off!"

The theme song of this here breed of heavies:

> *Grub for breakfast, lunch, and dinner.*
> *Grub for all the in-betweens.*
> *Grub for sunup, noon, and sundown.*
> *Grub until we split our seams.*

Sung to the tune of the gospel hymn about the blessings of deprivation for the children of the English working classes that Gramps learnt at Sunday school three hundred years ago.

Gramps and the lamentable parodies of his old age.

Marc fixing the clamouring mob with his bleariest eye. "Go chase a flounder. Go catch a crustacean. Go do what you like, but don't do it here."

Still swooping in from all points like a continuing rush of overfed humans to the bargain counter in the meat department. Glittering little eyes alight with gluttonous expectations. Without exception gorged to the gills already on everything boilable, burnable, bakeable, or deep-fryable. And beyond question having been fully occupied swallowing whole the throwaways since the first fisherman came ashore at daylight frying the pick of the catch on his little Primus stove.

"Oh, shove off. Go dig a mud crab. Go chase a minnow."

The usual couple of bully boys swaggering in advance of the front ranks, wings part-folded like knuckled fists, ready for beating up the more reckless members of the hoi polloi who might dare to step ahead of the mob when the bleary-looking human started dishing out the dainties.

"The menu, thanking you," squawked the bully boys, "to be uncontaminated by ham sandwiches with lettuce and pickled cucumber. And none of these here cream sponges either, with caramel topping. Let's have the genuine article, kid. The fish-and-chips leftovers. The good old-fashioned cracklings from the bottom of the grease-paper parcel. Which, as you well know, promote obesity and early death in humans. But health, strength, vigour, and prowess for us seagulls who don't give a damn if we die tomorrow as long as we're stuffed till we stagger with cracklings today.

"Further. Each personal serving to be tossed aloft fragment by fragment. Each toss-up the cue for another big performance from the quick-as-a-flash seagull *corps de ballet*. We're limbering up. One and all. As you can see. Us bully boys and the hoi polloi. Doing our exercises at the sand barre to the accompaniment of the overture."

Marc scowling. "Haven't you read the sign? UNDER NEW MANAGEMENT. Everything round here's for sale. Nothing's going free. Except sticks and bricks!"

Marc sweeping up a handful of sand and hurling it at them.

To the last feather a hundred and thirty-one seagulls rising like a regimental flag to a gust of wind. And at once alighting, no hard feelings, in the same pecking order, still pressing forward, still declaring the same expectations. The less well placed peering around corners or stretching tall to see above the heads of the bustling crowd.

"I came down here," Marc said, "to get away from it all.

I didn't come down to be bullied by a bunch of bloody
seagulls."

Groaning onto his feet, hitching up his duffle bag, leaving
the rowdies to consider the truth that the world wasn't what
it was and was fast getting worse.

No cracklings!

Not even the crust of a cucumber sandwich?

Something about telephones . . .

An improper thought causing Marc to blanch.

A rumour stirring in the back of his mind that public
telephones might have been invented and were possibly to
be found at the post office on the hill. Even arranged in an
orderly manner like ten little green piggy banks hanging
on the wall eager for small change . . .

Marc putting in his twenty cents. Begrudging it. At home
telephones were free, providing a fellow was quick on the
dial and greased lightning out the door.

Marc looking shifty. As if proceeding might precipitate
a national crisis and provoke a swift government crack-
down.

Marc grimly dialling the number.

Same old number. Same as always. Same old flutter in
the throat. The onetime magic number that for years and
years brought his lovely Gramps as close as a breath.

Remembering the sound of his grandfather's breath.

"Been into the claret again, Gramps?"

"I'll clout you, kid."

The ringing. The click. The other familiar voice.

"Hullo there."

Mark ripe and ready to faint.

Gran!

Talk about stunned plovers. Talk about going through your personal files in search of your voice . . . "Hullo, Gran."

"Marc . . . Marc! What's this about?"

Gran, if I were to take you up on that. If I were to tell you.

"Marc! Are you there?"

"Yeh, Gran . . . I'm here."

"What's happening there? What's the problem? Why didn't I hear the STD pips? Where are you calling from?"

"I'm coming early."

"That's nice. When am I to expect you?"

"In point of fact, Gran . . . I'm on the way."

"You don't mean today?"

"Of course I mean today."

"The arrangement is tomorrow, Marc. Tuesday. Three-thirty p.m. Tuesday."

"No, Gran. Today. Always Monday. Now even more so."

New storms gathering on Marc's horizon. Where'd she get Tuesday from?

"Three-thirty today, Gran . . . We talked about it last night. It's always been three-thirty today."

"Never."

"No question, Gran. Way back to last May when we arranged it. We sure haven't changed it. Tuesday was to be the day we started tripping around."

"Well, wherever you are, you'd better start tripping yourself back home. I've got things to do here. I'm up to my ears. I've got meetings. I've got ladies coming for tea. I'm going to dinner with friends. Today is not convenient. It was never meant to be today."

Marc saying nothing. Quietly breaking his heart. Too astonished to think of anything.

"Well," she said, "what's done is done, I suppose, as your grandfather used to say. I'm glad you've thought of letting me know. Or you'd have had a meagre lunch. I doubt if there's a thing in the house you'd want to eat. What time, then? What train?"

"Not exactly the train, Gran."

"Does that mean what I think it means?"

"The bus."

"Yes. I hear you say the bus. You'd better tell me where you are."

Oh hell . . .

"Look, Gran, I've got to run. The driver's on his way out again. He stopped for a dash to the toilet, I reckon. I thought I'd better call."

"None too soon."

"Well, I've done it, Gran."

"You've done it all right. I'll have to rush out for a few things or you'll be doing without your lunch. If I'm not back, you know where the key is."

"Thank you, Gran."

Hanging up the phone.

Looking blankly at the wall.

I blew it. She blew it. Did we ever blow it.

What's happened to her brain? There we were last night. There I was, telling her . . .

I can just see myself. Turning up here at three-thirty tomorrow. And everything sold. The big cash buyer answering the door: "Boy, the tradesmen's entrance is at the rear if you've come to clear the drains."

Of all the lousy, rotten, stinkin' tricks.

And all those lies about ladies and meetings.

Marc short enough in the breath to choke.

Sick enough to throw up.

Hardly able to hold back the tears in full public view of all those guys and girls passing by.

One more question.

When Gran's not at home to the kid on the doorstep, how come she's at home to the kid on the phone?

A flash of temper.

Marc running through the gate, past the shocking sign, up the cobbled path to the front door. Everything looking as before.

Raising the knocker Gramps brought back from Java and allowing it to fall. Listening to the impact cracking through the house. Raising it again and cracking it down. Raising it the third time. Cracking it down.

Indignation in his chest like an inflatable object.

"I was right. She's moved out and done us cold. Only thing I didn't think of: the phone. Took her phone number with her. Done the whole family cold, Dad included. No wonder she always came up to visit and wouldn't let us come down. And now she's done herself cold. Got her bloody days mixed. Her head spinning round. And no one telling me the house was to be sold because no one knew."

She said the key.

She said you know where the key is.

"I know where it used to be."

Marc stumping to the front end of the verandah, turning the corner out of sight of the street and clear of any vantage point the Forsythe sisters might favour.

Marc feeling under the windowsill with a forefinger. "It's here! I'll be damned."

SEVEN

Leadbeater and the Monumental Absence

MARC WORKING the key into the lock. Giving it the required number of jiggles. Hearing the operative click. But gripped by a feeling that the lock and key were energized. As if needles were about to run wild in his blood.

There was the door, drifting open, as if it might protest with a moan or a groan carried over from the wastelands in Marc's heart.

The moment holding Marc captive to the point of pain.

Marc peering into the gloom; the old familiar outlines taking shape. Everything in there seeming to be as it used to be. The smell of artifacts from deserts and kampongs and jungles. Not the smell of dust or neglect. The smell of rugs, and leather, and folk weaves. Of beeswax and polished woods. Even the smell of artist's oils on the unframed canvas hanging a few steps down the hall. The painting of Marc and the ocean at Nemesis, by Gramps, his last, carefully brought home and placed there five months ago. For some reason best not thought about, still smelling wet now.

Inferring that Marc was classified as a fitting, as a furnishing, and destined for the hammer in the hand of Miss Hudd and Sons.

Oh, it's a rough house that you're running, Gran. No holds barred. Even the air for breathing going under the hammer. Even the smells gathered from the whole wide world and brought home across oceans and through clouds. And then there's more to go under the hammer. Something that hasn't been here before.

Marc troubled again by a shortness of breath. A phenomenon having but little to do with anger. Or of running around the town. Having more to do with the gloom in there, with familiar shapes seen in a different way.

Something here was new. New in a sense you wouldn't want to know about. Something it might be proper to treat with caution. Something the human eye might never see. The kind of thought Marc wished to push aside. As if it came from the caves and the campfires and the howl of wolves.

Call the feeling upon the threshold unlike the feeling of anywhere else.

Best to back off. Best to get away.

But his sneakers wouldn't lift. Wouldn't shift. Were bonded to the mat.

Call it an alien stillness in there. An alien condition of life.

Call it the monumental absence of Gramps.

This is what it is. This is what it's about. The monumental newness of his monumental absence.

Nothing to draw Marc in. The once joyful house repelling him.

Nothing urging him to rush in along the passage. "Here

I am, everybody." For even when he'd come upon it, un-occupied, everyone was there just the same.

"Come on in, Marc. Make yourself at home."

This time: no invitation, no welcome.

This time: an intense inhospitality and in Marc the in-justice of a long-lasting moment of guilt that changed into fear of the open doorway, as if demons might rush out.

Marc in great trouble with shortness of breath.

Not wanting to know the shape or form or substance or anything about demons. Knowing only that the threat of them and the possibility were at this moment too believable.

Remembering, with a pang, Grandpapa in his splendour.

"You look like the Pope, Grandpapa."

"And you, insolent boy, look like an insect that might eat my books!"

Grandpapa. A hundred and three.

A daunting prospect. A family that lives forever. Except for misadventure. Or execution.

Grandpapa, the old-time prophet on the mountain. Still laying down the law upon matters of doctrine to all seeking his opinion. And to many who weren't. Grandpapa left in an uncaring world that had taken its new directions. A world not interested in his ancient language.

Grandpapa in years not long past (so the story has it) exorcizing the residence of a gentleman known virtually to all. The great man's wife having become a dangerous quantity in mixed company unless chaperoned by her psy-chiatrist. The great man afraid to enter his own library after 7 p.m. His children and grandchildren hesitating to stay for tea and not even under pressure agreeing to stay for dinner. Enter Grandpapa, the superpriest, with bell, book, and candle.

One of the great tales of the family.

Grandpapa driving out demons.

Next question. Perhaps an inner and invisible door blocked Marc's entry? A door of greater than visible substance beyond the threshold along the opening arc of the outer door?

Perhaps by stretching for this imagined door, something beyond imagination might come to his touch! Or enfold his hand and pull it into itself!

Marc's very own hand at the end of his very own arm, but not anymore to be seen.

The question becoming hysterical.

Marc developing pains in the chest.

As impassable as rock, this invisible door. Opening to a secret command or an attitude of mind. Otherwise closed. Against Marc. Against Hudd and Sons. Against Gran. Perhaps even against Grandpapa, the superpriest with bell, book, and candle.

An invisibility taking possession of this house and driving everyone out.

Hadn't everyone gone?

A compulsive but fearful raising of Marc's right hand. He thought of it as a testing of the water.

Stretching out with the hand, with great fear, and great pain, over the sill of the doorway, stretching even beyond his usual reach.

Sharply retracting the hand. Clearing his husky throat. Fearing the curious or amused or derisive attention of passersby.

Fearing the Forsythes atop their stepladders.

No one in view.

Heartfelt thanks to Grandpapa's God.

Marc swallowing hard.

Immediately in difficulty trying to keep his heartbeat down. Immediately having to admit he was sore with nerves and with feelings that had no name. And sore with persistent remnants of anger against Gran. And against Hudd and Sons. And against the exhausting worry of this incomprehensible door.

"It's a ghost in there."

Off the top of his head.

As if someone standing apart spoke the words.

As if syllable by syllable his own ridiculous response acquired the dignity of an important public announcement.

Like the town crier atop the city hall, arm thrust aloft in the grand manner, handbell clanging.

Hear ye. Hear ye. It's a ghost in there!

Marc trying to be rational, to be calm, but becoming even more keenly aware of a coldness that was becoming colder. Becoming even more certain that the difference inside this house was directed against him.

Which meant he was required to face it. Which meant he had to challenge it. Which meant he might need to rush in: "You can't be a ghost. You're my lovely Gramps. You've been part of me."

But was not Shakespeare, as almost always, the ultimate authority: the better part of valour might lie in discretion?

Might it not be wiser simply to shake a fist? Though might that be taken as provocative? Perhaps he should shake his head, inconspicuously, as if making little of it, as if to say, "Oh, my lovely Gramps. You can't be a ghost. It's not mathematical."

The act of putting it into words, the act of saying it, even inoffensively, left his spirit aghast.

It was true. As Marc knew. A man like Gramps, dying as he had died, was the old-fashioned stuff that ghosts were made of.

Though why should Gramps haunt the happy house?

Should he not haunt the terrible and unforgiving sea?

Marc standing there. Lost, to a degree. Sweat in his armpits. Wringing his hands. At the point of yelling through his gritted teeth, "I don't believe it. I won't." Then at the point of collapse. And at the point of rushing inside, attacking like a maddened creature, screaming and shouting and banging with his fists into the walls. And at the point of turning and running for his life. At the point of putting each impulse into instant effect, but stuck like mud on the mat.

Thinking back, distractedly, to conversations with Gramps. The teasings. The scoldings. The corrections of behaviour. The disputes. The presence. Though not the face-to-face and side-by-side and heart-to-heart presence of the good old days. Not thinking back to those days. Remembering the conversations that began within moments of the appalling understanding at Nemesis that Gramps was gone out of this life. That Gramps, like a plant at the end of its season, was dead. Leaving only the seed.

Appalling . . . The first moment in all of Marc's life that he knew what *appalling* meant.

So what could be wrong with making up conversations and not speaking them aloud? Just living them inside. Just easing the pain.

Gramps could have said, had he been there, "Very sensible. Why shouldn't you ease the pain? I wish I could."

But Gramps wasn't there; despite a quarter of a million reasons for his presence. This house—this extension of himself shaped by his own hands—going to a person or persons whose suitability began and ended with the quarter million reasons or the half million reasons or however many reasons the auction excited.

In exchange for them, Gran selling everything he'd ever made and ever owned. Even the top-heavy trees leaning on the house. And the tar on their wounds. The pigeon droppings on the ridge. The spiderwebs in the grille and the tyre gone flat. The Forsythes like puppets on their stepladders.

The lot, knocked down under the hammer in the eager right hand of the superbly painted young lady.

Selling the grandson also.

Now, what am I bid, in addition, for the boy? A hundred and ninety-two centimetres. A reasonable amount of boy. Or the grass will die. And the trees will drop their limbs. And the seeds will fail to show their heads. And the birds will never sing. He'll see to that. And the pigeons no longer will strut on the roof to crap enthusiastically. What am I bid? Feed him your leftovers. Keep him in the shed. Throw him a bag for a bed.

So perhaps Gramps had become the inner door. Had become the sentry. Barring Marc entry.

Perhaps, on this last day before strangers walked in, entering this house on any pretext was entering a sacred place. Not since Gramps had failed to return from the sea had Marc entered it alone. Not since the day of the funeral had he entered it at all.

The day of flowers heaped upon the empty coffin. The day of hundreds of persons he'd not seen before, except for the few with famous faces met from time to time in the TV news. The people who belonged to the wider life lived by Gramps, of which Marc had not been a part. Like discovering that the guy who lived next door was an alien from outer space, for when he took off his clothes, and his hat, and his head, nothing was there.

The hundreds of people, that day, commiserating with the grown-up family. None, it seemed, giving Marc more than a smile or an abbreviated thought. As if the kid had no real feelings. Having not grown into them yet. Or blaming him. Just one lady, on her own, passing by, touching his shoulder. No face seen. An electric touch. For a moment felt, then perhaps forever gone.

An awful day, bewildering day. The second most awful day of his life; coming so soon on top of the worst. And to cap it, the unveiling of the magnitude of the life that Gramps had lived of which Marc hadn't known.

Perhaps now, on this doormat, he should begin accepting that Gramps was the late Professor Emeritus Marcus Leadbeater. Followed by a list of letters as long as a telegram. Not Gramps at all. Not seriously. Being Gramps was a sideshow. Tolerated for a day or a week here and there. The part in which he played the role of Gramps being a back alley of life.

Marc had lived behind a paling fence along the back alley, along with the litter and the stray cats.

Perhaps, today, he had to start living with the things they'd said about Gramps. That aspects of the country could never be the same without the mathematical saint of the age. That without his reassurance the multiplication table might become suspect. And that Marc should now begin to accept the realities of respect for the dead by bowing his head. Or going down on his knees. Or beating his brow into the bluestone wall.

Didn't they know that in his heart he'd felt that way almost since he'd been born?

Perhaps he should try ridding himself of the remnants

of his anger, for Gramps had cherished Gran (Dad said) through a marriage lasting forty-two years.

"Do you know what cherish means, Marc?"

"Tell me, Dad."

"Perhaps there's no one who can. But if ever it comes to you, as giver or receiver, I believe you'll know what life means."

Dad in one of his greater moments. Another being his landing in Bangkok—three hundred and eighty-nine souls aboard—three engines gone and chaos after a lightning strike that came from beyond the world.

Imagine a kid losing sight of Gran's forty years of being cherished. Forty years like being forever. Like being the measure of the total time he might need to go on living with the mess Gramps left behind.

By comparison, Gramps had cherished Marc for hardly any time. But could anyone, even Gramps, cherish a clumsy kid with endless ailments from baby diarrhea to acne and seen once in a blue moon coming out from behind a paling fence down a back alley of life?

The tears breaking through.

"It's not my fault, Gramps. All this terrible trouble. I didn't drive you into the sea. You went down on your own. You said, 'Come.' And I refused. Three times I refused. It was my right to refuse. And how right I was or I'd be dead with you. No body to bury. Just a plaque on the cemetery wall beside yours. Would you really wish that for me?"

The door of the house still gaping open, the cold inside still laden with mysteries.

Gramps was sending him away.

What of the key left in the lock? The key now in reach only if he stepped across the threshold and jiggled it and wriggled it and with difficulty withdrew it.

"It can stay. Gran'll have to like it or lump it. I'm not going in there even for the key. I don't bloody care if the house is left open forevermore."

Oh, the monumental absence of Gramps.

Gramps, why are you doing this to me?

The stepping back. The tearing apart. The first deliberate step. The second. The agony of the third. The frightful and formal and final turning of his back.

The walking away down the cobbled path with the bottomless heaviness of heart.

The desolation of the open street.

Not the emptiness or aloneness of that street.

Oh hell.

There was an intrusion upon the street.

For there was the lovely Miss Hudd and Sons. Loveliness no longer meaning what it used to mean.

She'd said she had a name. It wasn't Jean. It wasn't Jane. Was it Jael? With a tent peg in her hand.

Miss Hudd and Sons, as if caught in a guilty act. Or poised, as if about to flee the scene, though having just entered it. And being so close to Marc he could have hit her, in his resentment, with the stretching flat of his hand.

"Marc."

"Oh, go away. What could I say to you that wouldn't get me locked up?"

"I want you to listen."

He was walking. He was moving. He was leaving her behind.

"Marc Leadbeater! You mustn't run from me."

"I sure don't intend to stay."

He was striding, long-striding, with the duffle bag and its contained sharp edges, and off like a runaway.

Was there anywhere to go?

Yes.

Round the corner to the right. Then the corner to the left. And on to The Little Jubilee.

———◆◆◆———

EIGHT

Leadbeater around the Corner

WHAT OCCURS around the corner being the more interesting part of life. The stuff of newspaper headlines, for instance. And she being the driver of the scarred Corolla encountered by Marc in a nearby street some short time before.

The quintessential small white cottage, she'd said, called The Little Jubilee . . .

Was quintessential a word or a unit of measurement?

And further, if a construction of bare bones crawling with savage black ants answers the door, speak up. Bare bones are hard of hearing . . .

A statement with truth in it, no doubt.

All told, a combination of curiosities here present which might reduce the status of this port of call to the harbour a ship in distress might hesitate to enter even in a storm.

Marc in no way hesitating. Thus indicating the status of the storm.

Number 226.

There it was on the gatepost.

There was the gateway.

In truth, more a hole in a hedge of well-fleshed plants standing tall with shiny leaves and looking like a hot day. *Enormicus japonicus*, in the educated opinion of Marc.

There he was, classifying the flora in less than an instant and pounding through the hole in the hedge, hurtling on in the hope that he'd left Miss Hudd and Sons at least out of sight. Which he probably had. For Miss Hudd and Sons, in the interests of good business, might wish with fervour to make peace or amends, but wish never, visibly, to make a spectacle of herself. Marc, on the other hand, having attained an age and an aptitude for making a spectacle of himself no matter whose expectations were involved, even his own.

Hence, panting behind the hedge, in his funk hole of shiny foliage, waiting for the pursuing clatter along the concrete pavement of the heels of the tiger.

Nevertheless relaxing to the first stirrings of satisfaction he'd felt since he'd hit town.

Satisfaction broadly based, as Dad might have put it.

Satisfaction that he'd not been clawed on the cheeks. That he'd not lost his head in her hearing and sworn to excess. That he'd not sprawled headlong and damaged various valuables attached. And that any improvement in the status quo, however slight, was in the nature of victory over Napoleon at Waterloo.

At this point it became reasonable to assume that the tiger with the luminous claws had not taken up the challenge.

Marc emerging with care, opening a little to the sun, attempting to suppress his wheezing breath and cautiously observing the situation he had so recklessly rushed in upon.

A distinct sandhill, domed, clothed in mown spring grass lying in erratically curved ridges. In his professional opinion, a job of mowing worth only a shudder. This area confined by a living palisade of ti-tree and *Enormicus japonicus*, each enjoying its usual vigorous and impenetrable growth.

Well, if it were not *Enormicus japonicus*, possibly *glossicus*. In any event, undeniably, *Japonicus whatthehellicus*.

Sited upon this untidy domed sandhill, some fifty, sixty, or seventy years (in Marc's expert opinion), a onetime fisherman's cottage of whitewashed cement brick and decaying timber trim, occasionally glimpsed over the years, though not with its new and incongruous roof of green corrugated iron.

Parked beside the cottage, the yellow Corolla bearing multiple scars at the rear end. The Corolla he had earlier brought to a stop in the middle of the street where Gramps used to live. That other street, from this new point of observation, becoming the street around the corner where the more interesting events of life occurred. The stuff of newspaper headlines, for instance. A moment of enlightenment.

And, in the same moment, appearing out of the sandhill like a hobbit, the woman in whom he had confided his sorrows. Marc noting, wholly from an aesthetic viewpoint, that she did not in any way resemble a construction of bare bones crawling with savage black ants. Nor, in any sense, a hobbit. And only vaguely resembled the face he had viewed through his tears.

Tears, obviously, being an instrument of severe diffusion and in future to be avoided in the presence of stunning women, for one might miss moments of promise.

Her name, he recalled, with embarrassment, might have begun with D. Or E. Or C.

Which could have made it Caroline. Or less likely Evelyn. Though (shades of the great Gramps crippled by the same disease) probably neither.

Which meant it wasn't Dora either.

"Marcus Leadbeater, I presume."

Though he feared her name could not be Stanley, nor his own Livingstone.

"Yes, lady. Leadbeater, Marcus R."

"You've accepted my invitation."

"Here I am, unless she catches up!"

"Your grandmother?"

"Miss Hudd and Sons. We had a difference. I left her at the house."

"Long may she remain there, for I'd be happy if you'd join me for lunch."

Wasn't that nice? A civilized introduction to life around the corner where one supposed that dreadful people lived and terrible things happened and you had to fight your way through roped-off areas and ranks of journalists and coroners and police officials.

Coyly, Marc said, "I don't know about lunch. I haven't had time to think of it."

"Why not think of it now?"

Not unpredictably, the state of Marc's health, his short-term expectations, and his brightness of eye began advancing at a pace. For this lady, for lack of a proper name, removed from the inner reaches of her chariot with scars, was seen to be a lady of exceptional aspect. As Gramps with a raising of the eyebrows might have put it. Though, scarcely a doubt, twice Marc's age, had the issue of age ever been worth serious hesitation between friends?

Surely all persons enjoying the same air at the same moment must be contemporaneous. Elementary mathematics. A typically Grampsian computation.

"Thank you. Lunch would be nice."

(Well accented, Marc thought. Pitch of voice, mature. The influence of Harwood Hampshire's School of Voice and Drama at last showing through.)

The lady said, "The name's Beatrice, for I'm reminded that the bringing to memory of any proper noun is a problem in your family. Would Doctor be less forgettable?"

Now she was teasing.

Marc (inner clearing of the throat) wondering if he had missed a point. From experience, he knew he probably had.

"Though not," she went on, "a sawbones. For which I offer thanks, repeatedly, in my dawn-time devotions. So proceed with caution, young man, for brickwork, uprights, and rafters hereabouts, to name but a few, are not to be relied upon. And in matters of first aid, neither am I. Injury, illness, and incapacity reduce me to hysteria."

"Yes, lady. Thank you, lady."

"Oh, come along."

Also spoken as if teasing. As if addressing a worldly fellow who'd know what the game was about. Which, regrettably, Marc didn't. Though, with a slow and graceful movement of the hand, *andante*, taking in the cottage, she suggested he should accompany her.

With an equally slow and graceful nod, and scarcely a stumble, he followed.

Doctor, she'd said.

Of what?

No straight hair gathered into a bun. No pinstripe suit. No BMW purring at the door poised for the next dramatic dash to the heart-transplant unit.

Nothing on offer except a beat-up Corolla. A shapeless sweater hinting at possibilities. And jeans frayed from honest wear and tear. And hair like a waterfall lit by a burning sun. Well, hell. What's life without a bit of poetry?

As for "coming along" in literal terms: take a look, doctor lady; here I trot. At heel. Star of the forthcoming Year Eleven musical, *Dracula Vernacular*, and now giving an impression of the vampire's faithful hound.

Woof.

Which, from a present perspective offered to this here hound (answering to Baskerville), leads him to conclude that your brilliance must challenge your beauty. That you must have zipped through the jungles of academia like a high wind. For how could you, otherwise, present this sweet deception of a mere twenty summers? My Gramps in some way that I cannot bring to mind must be the source of that.

This here hound, name of Baskerville, a Dalmatian. Kindly refrain from improper note-taking of the irregularity of the spots. His eager stumbling steps. His dizzy captivation.

(Momentarily, I give thought to what captivation once meant in a less kindly world. Custody, dear lady. In the coarsely knuckled fist of the school principal.)

Baskerville, out of modesty, feeling a compulsion to clear his throat.

Though why should it sound so strongly of *woof*?

The well-bred young dog must behave at all times in a gentlemanly manner. Particularly in the company of accomplished ladies. Or they may flatten him with a forearm jolt.

But the centuries-long reputation of Leadbeaters at large works against me, I fear. We are such a disreputable lot.

Recalling, notably, in the broadest of terms, my beautiful Gramps of loving memory. And other equally famous Marcus Leadbeaters beyond ready calculation. Even Grandpapa. Bishop. Commander of the British Empire; for services, it has been rumoured, to religion. Outliving three wives. Some witnesses suggesting four. Relating particularly to the first wife and the first year of theological college. About which I, and the Establishment, are believed to have no proof.

Dr. Beatrice? And not a sawbones!

Do I suspect that someone else has said the same thing at some other time?

The bell!

There rings the bell in the nave of mine head.

Accompanied by the shock.

Like the longed-for change of watch due at midnight coming on early in the middle of the storm.

Marc's heart missing a beat. His stride missing a step. His spirits leaving the launching pad, all systems GO.

Dr. Beatrice Campbell, B.Sc., Ph.D.

Who else can it be?

The infamous femme fatale!

From whose dreadful clutch it must, with luck, be too late to escape with dignity. For how can a fellow run from everything? To flee is unmanly, except from the likes of the glittery-eyed Miss Hudd and Sons with the luminous green fingernails.

Oh, what deplorable good fortune. That the bus home to virtue and honour has long since departed from every available street corner, for am I not entering The Little Jubilee? Is that not the name I spy upon the hand-carved hunk of pine screwed to the wall adjacent to my left eyebrow? Is not my personal foot, in the scruffy-looking sneaker on the matching left side, at this moment crossing the step and about to be followed by another?

Am I not more into this den of deliciously questionable reputation than out of it? This territory of the savage black ant given to reducing human constructions to fascinating bare bones?

Am I not following the infamous doctor of philosophy like the eager puppy, the younger Baskerville, if not in the full spirit or capacity of the mature and faithful hound?

Following along the narrow wired-in porch, again with scarcely a stumble.

Following into the small cluttered kitchen attached to the living room like the long left ear of the school principal.

Small kitchen smelling deliciously of items of pastry meditating in a warm oven.

Sink stacked with yesterday's dishes thoughtfully draining. For how could she have used this heap of rubbish since breakfast? Unless she dines in the company of circus elephants. Which I consider unlikely in view of the pack of Krispy Krackers with sesame seeds and the nearby platter of chicken-liver pâté with jellied brandy.

Observe the unopened bottle of Chardonnay.

Dewed from chilling.

In the company of two polished crystal glasses.

I'm expected.

This, take note, all you Year Eleven freaks, is how it's done in the real world. None of these backstage forbidden excesses. Here it is, all up front.

Woof.

Following on into the living room all but equal in breadth and depth to the volume of the house. Barely enough space

left in other areas—a rapid Grampsian-style calculation—
for the quiet place reserved for ablutions in general.

Momentary pause.

Consideration of ablutions. Considerations featuring the
fascinating bath in antique reproduction mother-of-pearl.
Sensually shaped in the form of the classic scallop shell.
Set about with teasingly transparent drapes perfumed with
Chanel. And old silver. And marble tiles.

Unless, following her devotions at dawn, the infamous
doctor dashes into the sea and quickly dashes out. Arousing
fevered observing in the hides along the clifftops established
by the Ministry of Lands and Conservation for the scrutiny
through binoculars of the flight and other mindless activ-
ities of *Larus pacificus*.

Music sounding in the background. As from the lady?

"Sit down, young man. Sit yourself there. And tell me
what this visit is about."

Friends, Romans, countrymen. Crowded living room.
With large and laden table in foreground for dining upon
sophisticated meals. For reflective afterthoughts and verbal
flirtations. For elegant writing upon elegant matters. For
being an infamous doctor at keyboard of computer packed
with startling computations and entrancing predictions
concerned with after-hours human behaviour. Together
with box of Oldacres Handmade Turkish Delight to sustain
mind, spirit, and constitution into the small dark quiet
hours.

Crowded living room with hard chairs in middle ground
for reading from numerous shelves bowed beneath weight
of hundreds of enchanting papers upon shocking subjects,
and thousands of books banned from schoolrooms and public libraries. To be found nowhere but here and in secret

vaults beneath the equally scandalous British Museum.

Crowded living room with worn red velvet settee for collapsing in at end of exhausting days of infamous research into infamous matters for the propagation of further delicious knowledge.

"Doctor? My fat foot. Doctor of infamy. That's what."

Gran's righteous pronouncement ringing through the silent halls of memory.

"Write your thesis on sin and they call you doctor! Doctor of witchcraft. Bewitching senile old men."

Which was rather rude.

My beautiful Gramps of loving memory leaving the scene through the mouse hole in the wainscot.

My young and tender forefinger to my brow.

Thinking this must be the recollection of a dream. But the conscious mind swears to its reality. Though there never was a hole in the wainscot. Even if there ever was a wainscot. Even if I knew what a wainscot was.

Crowded living room with sumptuous bed. Placed against farthermost wall in what must be termed a muted background.

"Marcus."

A voice like husky panpipes playing in the glen. Playing the tune of everyone's favourite name.

Lady, really. Lady, truly. This is your adoring hound. Your Baskerville.

Woof.

But here I draw a line. Does even a doctor of infamy need a bed muted as sumptuously as that?

"Bed. Is that what you call it? From rumours reaching me, it's what she brought from some Parisian bordello."

My very own personal mum's original utterance, a year

or two gone, intercepted at 01:36 hours according to the blushing face of my red digital clock, when she'd reckoned me past all capacity to intercept.

Dad hardly home out of Sydney, Singapore, Bahrain, Frankfurt, London, Frankfurt, Bahrain, Singapore, Sydney, Melbourne.

Budgie, answering to Factory Whistle, tucked in, his blinds drawn.

Cat, answering to Genghis, relegated to outer mat.

Front door on the latch.

"Did you lock the back?"

Somewhere, not far distant (conceivably in the present), the music of my name soothes me still.

Meanwhile, back at the farm, all the children also, bless our precious hearts, safe in the Land of Nod. Even old big ears, old well-known acoustic mine, a highly local synonym for me, alleged to awaken to the stifled popping of French Champagne corks (direct from Duty Free in Singapore), with five walls, four doors, and thirty-three feet of passageway intervening.

More music from the resident heavenly choir: "Please don't stand on ceremony, Marcus. All ceremony here is conducted from the sitting position."

One-thirty-six a.m. Even old acoustic mine in person known beyond doubt to be sound asleep.

Nothing, says Science Master Everest the Conquered, being less certain (ha ha) than when it is known beyond doubt!

That's when you get the nitty-gritty put together, my friends. Romans. Countrymen. Based upon crisp and crackling consciousness at 1:36 a.m. by the digital dial at the bedside.

Deny body, soul, and substance the longed-for sleep and

the world gives up its mysteries. The past makes sense and the future invites. ("Excellent paragraph in your essay, Leadbeater." English History Master Lev Poppov. "From whom did you pinch it?")

"Marcus Leadbeater!"

The music draws nigh. Indeed, draws nigher.

"Yes, lady."

"My settee is not a bear trap. Not a man trap. Not even a butterfly trap. I'm reasonably sure it'll not disable you."

"Yes, lady. Thank you, lady."

Marc sinking into an increasingly unlikely depth of threadbare red velvet and hissing goose feathers, clutching at his duffle bag for security, in fear that the scene could end in suffocation.

Was not suffocation to be counted a permanent disablement?

The voice of the temptress: "I promised you a drink."

Did she?

Had she promised Chardonnay?

I *couldn't* have forgotten *that*.

Marc striving to pull himself together while his duffle bag began to assume the stature of a block of concrete, bearing him yet deeper into an abyss of hissing goose feathers.

His breath wheezing again. "Oh yes, lady." Then with a gulp: "Thank you, lady."

Descent into bottomless abyss ceasing. No enduring symptoms of suffocation. Rather, Marc possessed of an urgent desire to run lightly, in bare feet, singing, along wet tidal sands.

Now she was speaking as if from an unscalable cliff, Marc at the foot.

"A point of order, Marcus. I'm of quiet and humble origin. If, in this town, we were cursed with a social register, my distinction would be my absence from it. You're making me nervous. Don't address me as lady. I haven't earned the distinction."

"I'm sorry about that, ma'am."

You see, I do have inside knowledge. I've heard the very same said of you in the company of my Gran.

"Neither must you address us as ma'am. I'm not the Queen of England. Though some of her anxieties I might enjoy. Her beautiful sons, for instance. Address us as Beatrice, if you wish to put us at ease. Or as Miss Campbell. Or, if your inclination is to amuse me, riotously, as Doctor."

"Yes, ma'am."

"You did say a drink? Am I right in supposing it may assist you to relax? No! On no account move! We will attend to everything ourselves. When one lives alone, one addresses oneself in the plural, though the rest of the world may consider us mad."

"Oh no, ma'am. Not exactly mad."

"Thank you, Marcus. That might be the nicest thing you'll say all day. An additional point: I require assurance that you're at least sixteen."

"Of course, ma'am."

"Are you given wine at home?"

"Oh yes. All the time."

"Are you an asthmatic?"

"No, ma'am. It's just that I wheeze when I'm emotionally disturbed."

"Marcus . . ."

"Yes, ma'am?"

"They call me Beatrice."

"And they call me Marc, ma'am. But they say it's a pet name. I'll be Marcus when I'm a full-grown dog."

Woof.

So she retired to the kitchen, leaving Marc to the labour of rolling first one eye in dismay, then the other in antici- pation, and finally both in what was probably another short-lived attack of primeval guilt.

———✦✦✦———

NINE

Leadbeater and
the Femme Fatale

THE VOICE of the infamous femme fatale issuing from
the kitchen. The music of her throaty tones sharpened by
the discord of her question.

"Ice?"

Lady!

In my wine?

I at once picture my father, a man of moderation and
virtue to the point of tedium: eyes dilating, stricken hand
clapped to his mouth.

My grandfather, neither moderate nor virtuous, yet of
mathematically sainted memory, would sink deeper yet beneath the wave.

My great-grandfather of notable antiquity and to this
very hour resident upon the holy mountain, unless gone to
his reward in the last twenty-four hours, would add unto
the law: *I give you the Thirteenth Commandment. Thou
shalt not associate with the like of Methodists who make a
virtue of watering the wine.*

Her face now appearing at the doorjamb. As if detached

and in need of a body. Any kind of body. Even a puppet's glove. For the moment reminding Marc of Punch, a role played in merest boyhood with rarest distinction. The Year Six breakup. Judy, spoken by the delectable Rosemary Richards, concealed from classmates and teachers, becoming hysterical with admiration and kissing him upon both burning cheeks, rendering highly improbable the more violent aspects of the performance as wildly applauded by the audience of cheering eleven-year-olds.

Then said the femme fatale: "Ice in your Pepsi?"

In my *Pepsi*!

Lady. What you do to my psyche. And my expectations. What you do to my fantasy life. What you do to your own infamous image!

The spoken word not delivered by Marc. The face saying it all.

"Pepsi, Marc." Coming from the lady in the nature of an affirmation. "For it's what you'll be drinking while you're here."

A long sigh from the poor lad.

"Oh, ma'am. That's like telling the actor on opening night that his play's been banned, the theatre's burnt down, and the agency's given him the push."

"I fear we haven't heard the truth from you."

"How could you, ma'am? Make a statement of the kind? Batting not an eye?"

"I don't believe you're sixteen. Sixteen fails to coincide with various matters that come to mind. And I'm certain you don't have wine all the time."

A gathering into himself of much breath. And controlled indignation. At last, after an unimaginably awful morning, a feeling of almost awful calm, as if the age-old spirit of the Leadbeaters had at last placed the hand of power and blessing upon his head. And the idea of Gramps having become a ghost of ill will might conceivably have been dreamt. And the feline Miss Hudd and Sons, at heart, was probably a nice soft pussy cat.

"Your information, ma'am, relating to age, is ill based, confused, or mischievous. Or all three."

A confident start. With a ring to it.

"At the most charitable it relates to an earlier condition, though I'm constantly and unkindly accused to this very day of acting like a ten-year-old. One inherits these tendencies to revert to childhood. What mere mortal can subject his genetic inheritance to prior and critical approval? What I am, I'm stuck with. Thanks to all the crazy mixed-up people who made claim to the Leadbeater name before they passed it on to me. Hence, I repeat, sixteen years and several weeks have I suffered the cruel barbs and arrows of misfortune as pertaining to these here latitudes. Unless me mum and dad have been monkeying with the facts in collusion with the Registrar of Births, Deaths, and Marriages. If they've been guilty of this irregularity, you can bet your fleecy-lined winter boots I'm older yet, for the margin between the nuptials and the arrival is as fine as you can get. Sixteen, ma'am, is the official statement, nonetheless. Certified by the bureaucrats. Their stamp upon my blameless and legitimate brow. Having most recently blown out the requisite number of candles at a quiet family function in the company of four female cousins, playfully inclined, but with an attendant and sinister surplus of long-nosed parents observing every move. Inhibiting the said cousins and requiring of me a second puff to extinguish the flames, with accompanying loss of face."

Marc wriggling his nose, which also was of more than moderate length. Wondering about the source of the lines.

From what play? By whom? By some enormously talented guy. Some star of stage, screen, and literatu-er. Like Noël Coward. Like Orson Welles. Like Leadbeater.

Continuing. Before the femme fatale had the chance to intervene: "Though I cannot swear to having wine all the time. I'm guilty, in this one regard, of marginal exaggeration. I have wine to celebrate the seasons. Which means I have it at Easter. Enough to wet the glass. Like a touch of autumn mist. And I have it at Christmas to celebrate the onset of the blistering heat. Enough to lay the dust at the edges of the goblet. And once I had it in a mug in the pantry with Rosemary Richards on the fourth of July. A real soak-up. To celebrate me mum's thirty-ninth birthday. While the alleged mature adults were singing songs riotously at the far end of the house. Words, ma'am, not entirely for the ears of the innocent like us. Entertaining. But disillusioning. Because did they get into us when we started singing our songs! Real harmless songs. Hardly even filthy. Former generations are not consistent, ma'am. It's as if they'd been born by mechanical means and granted instant adult status. No recollection of the hopes and joys and terrible deprivations of youth. I'd been telling myself you were the one to break the nexus."

"Am I," she said, "permitted at this point to voice a comment?"

"It's expected of you, ma'am."

"A comment indicating that I suspect I'm obliged to comply with your fevered wishes by demonstrating my celebrated wickedness?"

"On target, ma'am. I'm known among my peers as the Pious Monk. A great sadness. As you must appreciate. Can you blame a healthy lad, a patient sufferer, such as I, for a few pangs of boyish optimism that old Purity, Piety, and

Perseverance might be about to bust it for the new experience?"

Marc drawing numerous deep breaths to regenerate mind and body; the face of the femme fatale in the doorway having acquired a soberness.

"You," she said, "have the makings of the perfect scoundrel."

Marc nodding. Graciously.

"And possess a disconcerting adroitness with the tools of language. The like of which I've not heard since my last conversation with your grandfather."

"Thank you, ma'am. But I fear my mistress—my *English* mistress—would receive your comments with her strident derision."

"Dear Marc . . . Are you really going to waste yourself on the stage? Isn't there more to life than interpreting lines provided for you by writers and directors, the least of whom is likely to break the furniture over your head if you vary the script?"

"All Leadbeaters are scoundrels, ma'am. And all Leadbeaters are blessed with the gift of the gab. Embracing all at least back to 1066, when our noble forebear selling souvenirs adjacent to the battlefield at Hastings was approached by the Conqueror for directions to London. Our noble forebear's reply giving the Brits time to evacuate the city and escape underground. The eternal mark of the Leadbeater, ma'am, is loquacity. I think that's how you say it. With the exception of my father, the celebrated anti-scoundrel, the incomparable illiterate, the one flaw in the Creator's grand design. Never a blot on his copybook. Never mastered how to make a blot. Conducts all conversations in monosyllables and grunts. Me mum can trust him in any port of call on a round-the-world flight. At *his* age how tragic, as my Gramps with tears in his eyes used to say."

"Ignoring history, Marc, and thinking realistically of your father, what of the consequences to the pair of us if I give wine to you today to celebrate the coming of spring in September; even to celebrate your welcome appearance at this modest address?"

Another sigh from Marc. A warm sigh. With a sense of having arrived somewhere. A suspicion that his mighty engine had been missing on numerous cylinders until this encounter with the wonderful femme fatale.

"Ma'am, I do hope you're going to be my friend. To-morrow. Today. Forever."

The brow of the face in the doorway puckering. "I fear—indeed, I do fear—that it might be preordained."

"Then the present September's a real good month, ma'am, seeing you've raised this issue of preordination. Propitious for new enterprises. I read it in the horoscopes. You can trust me. Honest. I wouldn't breathe a word. Though I wouldn't go so far as to say that mum's the word. Or that dad's the word either. You know, at school they used to call me Highly Confidential. Now they call me Top Secret. And it's all depending on you, ma'am, and the Chardonnay, whether next year they'll be justified in calling me the Sphinx."

"Or the Sheik?"

"God willing, ma'am, though I'd hesitate to hope for as much."

"I repeat. The drink is soft. Ice in it? Or no ice?"

"Ice is for polar bears, ma'am. I like my lolly water, if I've got to like it at all, unadulterated."

She was looking him in the eye. Full and square, as if drilling holes. Slowly shaking her head.

"Hello, Marc Leadbeater. Hello, you. My goodness, you really are his grandson."

"I wouldn't know, ma'am. That's leaping to conclusions. This business of who you are and who you aren't is always to be taken on trust. Give it a moment's thought. Even allowing for scandalous misconduct at the Registrar's."

"I've been calling you Marc. Don't you think it's time to start calling me Beatrice?"

Marc swallowing hard on a spasm of genuine embarrassment and gesturing with one sweating hand from the depths of the red settee.

"I'll get round to it, ma'am, on a regular basis, at some future date. It's not that I'm anti-Beatrice or anything. It's a very elegant name."

An expressive sniff with a wrinkle of the long nose.

"Very historic. Very classical. But it's the way they brought me up. You'd think the pilot of a Qantas jet would be with it. But he's so old-fashioned. Straight out of the Brontës. Every man addressed as Mister, every boy as Master, and every unmarried female as Miss. Even if she's six. He ought to wear a Beaufort coat and derby hat and twirl a cane. Except that he'd look a twit in the cockpit and never live it down in the crew room. Here I am, barely embarked upon the quest to reach seventeen, and in knowledgeable circles, Years Eleven and Twelve, already called the Hilarious Hiccup of the Victorian Era, the one kid in no way equipped to cope with the modern world."

"I would suggest, young man, that you're superbly well equipped to cope with any world with a female majority."

The face disappearing from the doorway.

No sign of a body ever having been in evidence.

Not even a puppet's glove.

Very encouraging. Giving it thought.

Which went on to further reflection that he might even
yet have stumbled into a Central European fairy tale. When
she came back she really would be two feet tall, two feet
wide, and trailing a family of little hobbits clinging to her
skirts.

Back she came, looking cool and fantastic in the same
frayed jeans and not wholly shapeless sweater. When you
gave it sly inspection. Looking like someone else's older
sister who might not be averse to a bit of horseplay with
a likely lad.

Coming back with brandied chicken-liver pâté on Krispy
Krackers and two straight lolly waters in wineglasses. And
another jarring question: "How much longer are you to
going to embrace that wretched bag like a favourite kissing
cousin?"

Lady!

Marc in shock.

"Ma'am, you descend to language that must be declared
non sequitur. In local circles, I'm known as the Politician
Who'll Never Win a Seat, for I decline to kiss even the
blameless bottoms of little babies. Hence, I have no favourite kissing cousin. You'd understand better if you saw
my many non-kissing cousins. Beauty in the Leadbeater
family, ma'am, is not a strength among the females. They're
why the Leadbeaters travel so far from home and have
become such scoundrels. And this here honourable bag,
ma'am, to which you have most unkindly referred, contains
a number of private items of value, none affordable or
replaceable on what is laughingly termed my budget and
financial viability. It's also my security blanket. I used to
have a Teddy bear called Wee Wee. I apologize for that,
but it was not polite to say poo in our house. But how
could you call a Teddy bear number two? Or big job? Then

I had a green handkerchief with a knot in it. Now I sling my purple dilly bag and all's supposed to be well. Today my dilly bag, for some dreadful reason, has been letting me down . . ."

Suddenly a break in the mood.

"Bea . . ."

A catastrophic break in the mood.

A welling up of grief beyond control.

Marc not knowing where to look. Not knowing what to do. Wishing only to be home in bed with the blanket over his head.

"Give me the bag."

He allowed it to go and from there descended into a silent, shaken, and shaking world.

After a time she sat herself beside him, sinking against him into what he suspected to be the oceanic depths of the red settee.

Everything being related to the unforgiving sea.

Marc being less aware that an arm had lightly closed about him, but not ignorant of the hand mopping at his face with a handkerchief, or a tablecloth, or a bedsheet, or something coming off the roll by the metre.

In part he knew he was saying, "Isn't it enough that he should drown? And that she should sell his house? How could he turn into a ghost as well and drive me from the doorstep that he meant to be mine in the end?"

Then he knew she'd gone, but almost as suddenly knew she was back.

"I know, Marc, more than you'd suppose."

So he appeared to be crunching on a Krispy Kracker with brandied chicken-liver pâté. And sipping from a glass. All in between shortages of breath and further snifflings.

It wasn't Pepsi in the glass.

Her voice: "Easy . . . It's a little wine and a lot of fizzy lemonade. I don't know about you and wine; I can't believe a word you say. But I know you're not ready to drink anyone under the table. Now tell me why you're here, my dear friend. Tell me what it's about."

Marc sitting there. As if suspended in a condition of no gravity. Like not having been born yet. Coming together piece by piece. A few important pieces reluctant to stick on. Sipping from his very interesting glass. Savouring the pâté on his fourth Krispy Kracker.

"They cook the brandy out of it," he said, "don't they?"

"There's a rumour to the effect."

"It's very good."

"Then enjoy it while you can. Your doctor will be telling you soon enough to stick to the straight cracker and the glass of straight water."

"My great-grandfather doesn't stick to crackers. And reckons that water's for ducks. In some things he's not original. He's a bishop. And a hundred and three. He's outlived three wives. Some say four. The ducks that go for water, he says, run the risk of contracting foul diseases. Water, he says, was the eleventh plague of Egypt, and probably the source of the other ten."

"I know about your great-grandfather."

"He lives on a holy mountain. The local people call him Thor. At the cathedral they call him Bluebeard. In our house we call him the Holy Father. I think of him as Moses in the Clouds. He's a kind of freak."

"Far from it, my friend. He's quite a guy. Why did you cry?"

"Don't ask me yet, Bea . . . Please."

An uncommonly long pause. "Now you've called me Bea for the second time. Why?"

A silence from Marc almost as long as her pause. "Well, isn't it what he called you? May I have another glass, please, of this very nice lemonade?"

"You'll get us both into trouble."

"You're pouring it, ma'am. I'm the child victim of the wiles of the femme fatale."

"Marc, that's not fair. I'm a quiet country girl."

"I know," Marc said. "The Girl from the Golden West. The noise capital of the world. You used to work the juke-box in the Sin City Bar."

"Marc. That's not true."

"Someone we both know reckoned it was."

"Then he was a scoundrel."

"That's my lovely Gramps."

She went away. She came back. She placed the glass in his hand.

"Same as before?"

"You'll ruin me."

"No, ma'am. Leadbeaters never kiss and tell. Only in their memoirs. Same as before?"

"It's the second glass. That's the difference. Which makes it twice as bad as the first."

"Depends upon your point of view, ma'am. About whether it's twice as bad or twice as good. Thanking you very much."

"I'll end up in gaol."

"I'll visit you."

Marc sitting there enjoying his second lemonade and getting round to his sixth Krispy Kracker with brandied chicken-liver pâté.

"Do they really cook the brandy out of this stuff?"

"I confess, Marc, I haven't any idea."

"So I really can get sloshed on it?"

"I hope not. I'd imagine the brandy waved a finger from a distance and was whisked out of sight."

"So why do they call it brandied chicken-liver pâté? It's misrepresentation. It's a case for the Minister of Consumer Affairs."

"Enough, Marc!"

"Why, ma'am?"

"You're ruining me!"

"Not me. Never."

"I used to hear that from your grandfather."

"He didn't ruin you, ma'am. Never a word. Not even to me. And I was the litter bin at the end of the lane. And if he ever wrote his memoirs, he never left them lying around. If you got ruined, it happened some other way. Like Gran running over the odds. Or the two next door hanging over the fence. Ruining you would be nothing to them. Gramps used to say there never was a day they didn't ruin in some little way."

The femme fatale looking at Marc curiously. Even shaking her head.

Marc continuing to sip on his second lemonade.

"Ma'am, I hesitate to draw your attention to an invasive perfume. It's not seaweed and it's not *Enormicus japonicus*. I'd say it was hot pastry about to burn."

TEN

Leadbeater
at Lunch

MARC, WITH a strained expression, rising from the depths of the red settee.

"An unwelcome development, ma'am. The bathroom, please. If you don't mind."

His request coming in a thin voice, as if projected from a ledge at a great height. This being a further admission that despite the wondrous gift of the gab he was not cast in bronze in the classic heroic mould.

The hour having at least passed 1:00 p.m. and the afflicted body having left home at 7:38 a.m., following orange juice, cereal with milk, two fried eggs, and three breakfast mugs of tea.

"The bathroom?" she queried, as if moved to disquiet. "Back to the entry, if you must, and on to the bitter end." Followed by a sigh and what had to be seen as an apologetic shrug.

Marc waddling off to the "bitter end," which proved to be a hole in the wall concealed behind an unlikely door of hand-rubbed hardwood planks of enormous weight. The planks butted up to each other with the suggestion of a gap for the convenience of Peeping Toms of the insect kingdom. But once past the door!

A zone of iridescent pink and shades of unmatched green perfumed like a rose garden on a still night!

Marc thoughtfully, though thankfully, poised above the grass-green toilet bowl, considering its great age and the wreath of briar roses adorning its glaze. And giving thought to the lettuce-green washbasin with rust stains in the cracks. And wondering about the reliability of the large galvanized shower-rose looming like a rain cloud above the claw-footed and alarmingly deep bath. Each unit in communication with the Water Board via the fully exposed plumbing weaving wildly about the room like scribble on walls.

Backstage with the femme fatale!

Friends, Romans, countrymen. With respect I frame the following observation: no wonder her apologetic shrug.

Marc's attention then drawn to the toiletries and cosmetics occupying a narrow pine shelf well below his eye level. All containers bearing neatly hand-scripted labels: *Rose Geranium. Handmade by Sadie the Scented Lady.*

Rose Geranium for many and varied purposes. Rose Geranium A. Rose Geranium B. Up to Rose Geranium G.

Nothing on show relating to anything formerly noted by Marc in his mother's *Vogue*. Or allowed entry to his own shower recess, where he braced, twice daily, to invigorating onslaughts of much too hot or much too cold, tempered by brisk steppings-aside for vigorous soapings-down and brisk steppings-back-in. Hence turning with distrust to the bright pink soap. Rose Geranium X? Seemingly once eased by Sadie from the mould of a full-blown rose.

Marc defensively twitching his nose.

Then observing, and utilizing, the guest hand towel with embroidered pink pelicans. Or penguins. Or possibly sea-gulls. Probably originating from the Surf Lifesavers Ladies Auxiliary Street Stall last Easter Saturday morning just before the weather changed and the gales roared in from the sea.

A moment or so of recollection.

Gramps and Marc pausing to purchase the caramel sponge dessert especially baked by Mrs. Désirée Fitzpatrick in the famous oven of her renowned black iron wood-fire stove.

For Marc, with the towel in his hands, it became a moment or so of pain.

"Mrs. Fitz," Gramps said. "Salutations."

"Professor Leadhead. A pleasure, as always, to embrace you."

"Not today, madam. It's the child. He carries tales. When my wife comes by, Mrs. Fitz, you are not to discuss the square of fabric defaced with abominable pink objects, or I shall have you before the Vestry on an indecency charge."

"Your long-suffering lady's collection of hand towels and bathmats reflects my own impeccable taste. So get you about your business or there shall be *no* caramel dessert embossed *Big Leadhead* ready for you next year."

So be it.

Marc returning from Easter Saturday morning to brief consideration of the bathmat.

Pink porpoises upon the bathmat. Or possibly pink pterodactyls among clouds of emerald green? *Three* ladies in town with the same impeccable taste!

Marc peering then into the gothic-shaped mirror, the

view of himself being the ultimate offence against taste of
any kind.

The kid with Technicolor spots. The kid with Technicolor eyes. The tear-marked kid smeared across a background of iridescent pink and unmatched greens.

The delectable Rosemary Richards wouldn't have owned
him, despite their dazzling performance, Year Ten, in *Brig-
adoon*. An unrehearsed moment of joyous physical contact
on stage. The delectable Rosemary hissing into his shirt
buttons, "You'll ruin my good name, Leadbeater man."
Piercing whistles, meanwhile, of rapturous approval from
the mob.

Now, in the bathroom of the infamous femme fatale,
Marc launching upon a patch-up job.

Thus, perfumed with unavoidable items of Rose Geranium, self-consciously coughing into the fragrant palm of
his left hand, coming to take his place at the lunch table
opposite the lady, next to the silent but probably alert
computer.

"Well?" she said.

"I'm sorry, ma'am. Especially if I need to be."

"It's true I feared you'd lost the way."

"Time only, ma'am, to meet the needs and accomplish
the deeds."

An explanation emphasized by Marc with a blush and
the afterthought that anything added to reduce its precision
would make it more exact.

"Relax, Marc. We're all one in the flesh. Even monarchs
and presidents and little ones unblemished by sin."

"Ma'am. You're flogging it a bit."

"I'm noting," she said, "that the young man sounds more
like himself again."

"As ever, ma'am, the Leadbeater aim is to please. Though your kind observation gives rise to one in return. You've not known me long. I'm a mess most of the time."

"I think not. And how unobservant of you. How old were you when you first passed my gate? Old enough for Grade Four?"

Marc thinking about it.

"I know well the sunny boy who used to head for the surf. Aged eight or nine. And eleven and twelve. Followed by the brash interval and the trail of Coca-Cola cans and cigarette butts. Now, you assure me, you're sixteen. And grown-up. How *could* you for so long be unaware of the lady's approving eye?"

Marc giving even more thought to it.

"Maybe a guy reaches an age, ma'am, when he starts noting what constitutes a lady. Not just her good breeding, so to speak. So I apologize for the unaccountable delay. Or, like they say at home about the hound next door and me, perhaps I'm only a puff of woof. Spent my life in the shadow of the fence. Seeing only the fence. Failing to observe the wonders of the world. Take the fence away and I fold. Like the hound."

The lady shaking her head; critical lines crinkling the corners of her eyes.

"Marc, I do admit the pain, but cannot see the point of what you say."

"Obvious to me, ma'am."

"In that case I must ask you not to repeat it. If you're to be a philosopher, be sure of where you stand."

"If you say so, ma'am."

"That's flippant and unworthy of you. You offend your grandfather and do yourself an injustice. You libel some poor dog who can't speak up for himself. And I add, you should never carelessly jest at the expense of *Canis fami-liaris*. For you may not know what you do."

The lady having acquired a look more often seen upon Frau Zobel at desperate German coaching lessons after school.

"Never think of the figure of your grandfather as a negative kind of shadow over you. He loved you and lived for you and literally put you before all."

Just as well Marc wasn't seated upon the bottomless settee, or he'd have sunk. Truly people were not as subtle in his company as he felt they ought to be. Gramps had had the same trouble.

"Lunch," he then heard her saying, "you see before you. Tensed for demolition. Home-style low-cal low-fat sausage rolls spared the ultimate indignity of burning thanks to your patrician nose . . ."

Patrician?

My nose?

"With home-style salt-reduced sugar-reduced tomato sauce, pursued, for comic relief, by something tacky called Healthie Danish Pastries. All for flushing down with de-caffeinated coffee and soybean cream. Acquired from Gertrude's Gourmet Delicatessen at devil-may-care cost."

Marc reviving to this welcome change of climate.

"You really did expect me."

Forcing himself to say it with brightness, for he had to concede it wasn't scintillating stuff.

"To the contrary, young man, by arriving you amazed me."

Marc's spirit at once going pale again. His voice going pale with it. "But you invited me."

"Life begs courtesies, Marc. One needs to offer courtesies and receive them. One needs to acknowledge them and be thanked. When I've held a door open I confess to a wound when any person barges ahead of me without a glance."

Something in Marc's heart, both sad and joyful, that had revelled in her company was slipping away. "But you made such a point of asking me to come."

"One asks in hope, Marc. Truly, I didn't expect to see you. If ever again."

"Then I shouldn't be here."

Grownups rarely meant what they said. Even when they wrote their wills in favour of the ones they loved and lived for and put before everything else!

"Oh, my dear young friend . . ."

Shall I, he thought, turn out to be the same? When does the rot set in?

"Believe me, Marc, the royalties of my books don't allow me to lunch like this every day. I drove on round the block. Back to the shops. To be ready to celebrate in case you came."

Where was the trip wire hidden?

"Why be so unsure? Why be so sharp and accomplished, but so young and immature?"

For Gramps it had been the same. All those people leaping onto their high horses and galloping off. Caution telling him to be silent. To give his brain time to catch up. But how many more times was she to get off scot-free?

"Were you really his femme fatale?"

She flinched. "I gather that 'mistress' is the word you mean?"

"I wouldn't have said it, lady; but you did."

In the same moment he was stricken. In the same moment he was telling himself, "It couldn't have been me. I could never say a thing like that. It was never my business what Gramps did with his time or with whom."

"Scarcely his mistress, Marc. His protégée. One of many."

Marc's resentment raged. "Now what are you on about?"

Her voice rang. "You have a fault, I think."

Her eyes flashing.

"You have a *vice*, I think. A reluctance to listen and an eagerness to interrupt. You've asked an exceptionally cruel question and obstruct my answer."

Marc burning with shame, for he truly must have missed a word or a point.

"Attend to what I say, for it's not easily said. Allow me to know it was my privilege to be the last of his protégées. Hence it became my misfortune, about which I'm sure you've heard more than was true. Or good for you. Not only his protégée but his victim. I was too close to home and too inexperienced to know. The one judgement I make is that he should have known and should have been more discreet."

The fire in Marc, ever ebbing, or flaring, was more than he could hold down.

"That might sound good to you, but I've been hearing things like it all day. Everyone pulling the wool over my eyes. Even Miss Bloody Hudd telling me to get lost unless I brought a grownup with me. Am I five years old?"

"If you want to be heard, you must allow others to be heard. You were not the only one to associate with him or to love him."

"It's like a game the way you people push words around. Push 'em here. Push 'em there. If one line doesn't work, you try another."

"There was an urbane young man charming me some time ago. I can't imagine where he's gone."

"You ought to know. You're the psychologist."

"Love's on many levels, Marc. Your grandfather had a love for his students as well as his love for you."

"What have students got to do with you?"

"What do you think a protégée is?"

"Lady, I can't look all these different ways at the same time. I think I'll skip the lunch. I'd choke."

She flushed and banged her hand onto the table. "You're not walking out on me on top of that! You'll not leave me with that. You'll not do it to him or to me. Your Gramps gave me the special love he gave his special students. I owe my doctorate to him, and I'll wager that I wasn't the only female among us who nursed a few girlish hopes. You degrade my hopes."

"You were never his student, lady."

"Who told you that?"

"Everybody."

"Who's everybody?"

"Everybody."

There were shadows where the flush in her cheeks had been.

"Gramps was a mathematician."

"That's not relevant. You hope to be an actor. What have you been in your better moments but his student?"

A tiredness was wearying him. The day had become too much. Too much behind. Too much ahead. She was talking still.

"The loves of grown-up people become more complicated as time goes by. As you'll be learning, Marc. But nothing that your grandfather and I shared would need to be hidden from you now if you had but half a brain and half a heart.

"Of course I loved your grandfather. As incongruous as it may seem to you. Might have seemed the same way to him. How many years were there between us? Gossip, he said, was a prop of life for those who were not self-supporting. I've thought of less generous definitions since then."

Marc wondering vaguely what was incongruous and what was not, for his own image of himself was fading.

"When you were in town," she said, "you were his priority. Nothing was more important than the young Leadbeater. When you were at home with your family, he attended to lesser matters."

She could have been crying. He might have been crying, too. The quality of her voice changed.

"We ask a blessing on this celebration of a new friendship shared by us who loved our dear Marcus Leadbeater and need the comfort of each other, for heaven only knows how much more of our lives tomorrow will bring to an end."

These perplexing echoes faded and his head came slowly into contact with the edge of the table.

ELEVEN

Leadbeater
at Rest

POSSIBLY A happening. Possibly in the dark and seen within the heart.

At the table, Gramps and Marc. Situated light-years distant and light-years apart.

"Celebrating an ancient institution," Gramps explained. "The enjoyment of the hearty breakfast that comes the way of the happy condemned."

"Condemned?" Marc's voice going up the scale. "For what condemned?"

Gramps expounding: "First they waken you. For it is night. Then they feed you. Handsomely. Then, at a pleasant social function, you are presented with your operational orders; not infrequently by fetching young women in the uniform of officers of the Royal Air Force. Then, courteously, others convey you to your elegant killing machine and batten down the hatches. Confining you, as it were, to the interior of your pressure cooker. Whereupon you commit yourself to the fires of hell for the beguilement of the gods."

Marc's increasingly incredulous feelings breaking into a cry. "Man. That war was an age ago. The world was hardly formed. What have I to do with that? Marcus the meek, they call me. Marcus the mild. Who'd condemn to death a mere child? What have I done, ever, but suffer? You ask my mum. Where's my hearty breakfast for the happy condemned?"

Gramps sipping from a container of chicken soup with noodles, or the available equivalent. Provoking Marc to a further question: "How come, old spook, you've got that jug of stuff and I've got nothing but an empty gut, an empty plate, and an unused spoon?"

As this also begged an answer, Marc added, "Observe, no fried eggs. No fried potatoes. No muesli flakes. No hot buttered toast with yellow box honey. No Chardonnay in frosted glasses. All reasonable fare to put before the happy condemned. If Valhalla doesn't look better, I'll be lodging a protest with my Member of Parliament."

Gramps wearing a blindfold. In no way helping Marc to a better frame of mind. A demonstration, perhaps, by the mathematically sainted grandparent of miraculous powers acquired in heaven. As if to say, *Who needs eyes?* Related to the vanity of the vast moustache with curled ends worn by the same character during World War II. (A sensation, according to legend, among the young women of the day. A moment of thought centred upon the nature of the sensation.) A moustache familiar to Marc from pale photographs he'd once believed to have been posed against a painted background in a fun parlour.

Marc still presiding over his empty plate, a perfect commentary, he reckoned, on the quality of life.

"They feed you handsomely, you say? Who might *they* be, old spook? They're getting at you. You've been indoctrinated."

Gramps now working with one finger at one ear as if attempting to dislodge an obstruction. Possibly a spent bullet left over from the prehistoric era of vast moustaches. Then working with the opposite finger at the opposite ear. Shaking his head between. Water splashes, with sand and seashells, spattering across the table.

Marc not much impressed by this development.

"You're incurable, old spook. We've got names for show-offs. If they really have let you into heaven, don't get too excited. They'll be turfing you out soon as they wake up that some dumb clerk in Reception has read your papers wrong."

"Insolence, little man, won't advance your cause this day!"

"What cause? What day? And why call the truth insolent because it doesn't please you?"

Marc now aware that the only solid objects in view were the tabletop and two plain chairs. Like the stage setting for a scene in which only the words counted. The backdrop being another matter: galactic renderings of incredible darkness and incredible light.

Said Gramps: "The introduction of side issues will not be tolerated."

Marc now concluding that his outstretched feet were nowhere touching the floor.

Man, I'm a hundred and ninety-two centimetres tall! How long are the legs of this chair?

Don't tell me I'm on the scaffold. Don't tell me the beggars have cheated me of my last request! I take the appropriate breath. I shout. I want my Grandpapa, in person, in full regalia, to say the prayers and cast out the demons, leaving me at home tucked up in bed, never having got out of it this morning.

How come I can't hear myself?

Who's got my voice?

So Marc drew another extraordinary breath and went on to address the subject of side issues. "Do you call haunting the house you gave me a side issue? Do you call scaring me off the doorstep you directed me to maintain in good order and condition for the rest of my life a side issue? I quote. I quote from the letter appended to the crazy document.

External timbers to be repainted every third year by the unaided hand of the heir. Internal timbers to be hand-waxed by the same party. No structural alterations or additions, except for the accommodation of surplus wives, concubines, and children. No chintz chair covers, velvet curtains, wall-to-wall carpets, compost bins, or ponies associated with his younger daughters are to be permitted indoors.

"Do you call a damn-fool letter like that a side issue? Do you call giving everything away twice a side issue? What surplus wives? What concubines? What younger daughters? The only female I've ever seen is my sister Beth, and that was by accident and in her bath, and she damn near took me eye out with a squirt of shampoo."

Gramps apparently having moved to some other address, leaving his spectre behind to work at its ears. The components capable of speech having withdrawn to consider the mathematics of the beautiful ladies of generations past who might or might not have responded to his propositions of concubinage.

Godfathers, Marc then said to himself. Now I know why I can't reach the floor with my feet. There isn't a floor. No ceiling either. And no walls.

Which is the same as saying that once you're in this damn place there's no way out, because you're not anywhere at all.

"Leading me, old spook, to direct your attention to the ruination of the reputation of your femme fatale. This *lesser matter*, as you had the gall to call her. The lovely lady I'd be going for myself if I had the cheek. Which wouldn't be as *incongruous* as your going for her. How can you call her a lesser matter when she's had to take all your flak? And everybody else's flak? Then put up with mine as well? I'm so ashamed I don't know what to do with myself. And whose fault can it be but yours?"

Marc at the same time thinking: If there's no way of getting out of this mess, how come I got into it? This could be deadly serious. Along with what's happened to my hearty breakfast. Along with the granting of my last request relating to Bishop Marcus Leadbeater, C.B.E. And, further, how many beautiful young women really did fall into the clutches of this disgusting old spook?

Marc pursuing the line of thought. Relating it to life ahead. Life a lovely bunch of grapes. Every grape a beautiful young femme. Like the femme fatale. Like Miss Gorgeous. Like the eyes passing him by on the street. Like the delectable Rosemary, whom, let me say, I've loved day by day since I was seven. Faithful to her in thought, word, and deed. Certainly some of the time. And loving her in the most gentlemanly manner all of the time. A most regrettable streak of cowardice. Except in the pantry that fourth of July when me mum turned thirty-nine. And on stage in front of fifteen hundred yelling yahoos who cramped my style, but made it possible just the same.

Gramps saying, "About the sea-serpent . . ."

Marc exploding like a firecracker.

Friends, Romans, countrymen. The return to consciousness of the sainted ancient. *In the company of guess who?*

"You and your impossible old sea-serpent, old spook, are what the rest of the world calls extinct! And what I call too bloody much, on top of everything else."

Gramps removing his left forefinger from the matching ear and giving himself a vigorous shake. The rattling of bones and the clanking of anchor chains accompanied by splashings across the table of water, sandstone fragments, clam shells, and sea anemones.

Gramps then proceeding to point with the available forefinger in the general direction of what might have been a supernova. Or a flight of angels on a wild night out painting the town red.

"Hark," said Gramps, "do I perceive the distant bark of Marc? The adolescent lout. The well-known lack of form. The witless shout. Project the voice. Articulate."

Gramps poking the finger back into the ear.

Marc's firecracker reverberating on.

"Will you take the blasted blinkers off your eyes!"

Gramps giving the back end of his head a scratch.

"I's as the plural of me or the singular of you have nothing to do with the issue. I decline to associate with the grammatically diseased."

Marc feeling like leaping to his feet and doing the old spook in. Except that in the absence of a floor it might end in some horrible catastrophe. Like falling through the hole in the bottom of the universe.

"You can't go on like this when you're dead. Just count the friends you lost when you were alive. People with only half a brain can't stand it. Are you aiming at adding me to your list posthumously?"

"When the sea-serpent beckons, unquestioning compliance is required of all parties."

Marc poking his right forefinger into his left ear and giving it a spirited twist.

"I apologize, friends, Romans, countrymen, for aping this here gorilla and his tricks, but something must be wrong with my equipment. I'm hearing signals he was transmitting when I was six! Look, old spook, what's the big attraction about bouncing lifeless along the bottom?"

"Your boots, child, must be covering your head. Nothing reaches my ears but mumble. I spell out the future. Today we resolve the one issue we failed to resolve in life."

Cracked bells ringing inside Marc.

"I've heard this before. Did it make me walk into the sea with you, then? Though you damn near ordered me. And you know what I said! Do I have to say it again?"

"If that's your recollection, why do you question that you're condemned? We go down to the sea-serpent together. Allowing me henceforth to rest in peace. On the other hand, the two of us could consider the grand tour of the Clouds of Magellan presently available at the cut rate."

Marc sinking.

"Old man, you must know that all the people were saying it was my fault. Like saying Pompeii was my fault. Like saying I caused the Deluge."

An exhaustion beginning to sap Marc.

"The day of your funeral I heard it all in my heart. You must've heard it, too. No one there talking to me. Not even my dad there to hold me up. My dad in bed in bloody London with a virus."

The exhaustion sapping him more and more.

"Now they'll say I drowned myself. They'll say I couldn't live with myself. How can my Gramps do that to me?"

Marc trying hard to find words.

"And what of my Rosemary? Would you have me die without a real live clinch? And you being the expert on the clinch. She'll be thinking when I'm washed up that I never could have loved her except on stage or when I was in the pantry half-sloshed."

Gramps absorbed by explorations of his left ear.

Marc flaring: "You listen good. I had no contract with you. I was fifteen and hale and hearty and healthy. Would I enter into a death pact with someone seventy-four years old? You might get me, mate, when I'm a hundred. When I'm not looking. But you'll need to be quick."

Gramps sipping from his breakfast, whatever it might have been.

Marc yelling: "Never as long as I live am I going back to that place. Except the once with Gran. The very idea's been hanging over my head for months, like I was going there to get hung."

"A hanging, you say?" Gramps showing interest.

"Gran going to a hanging? Taking her knitting? And her knee rug? And her binoculars? I always reckoned she'd been born out of her time. Or is she the party due to be hung? Am I right in assuming I heard the name of Gran in this context?"

"You know what you heard! You know I came down here to go out there with her. Have you given any thought to that yet? Of what it was going to do to me? Then walking into that terrible notice stuck up by her and Miss Hudd and Sons. Have you any idea?"

"Can this incomprehensible mumble be issuing from the Leadbeater in whom the hopes of the gods of theatre have so fondly resided?"

Marc filling with tears. "I'm warning you. I really will do you in, old spook. It'd be dead easy with the mean streak you passed on."

Gramps removing his fingers from his ears and flexing his hands as if about to undertake a surgical procedure. Then removing the blindfold.

Marc crying out. Covering his face.

Said Gramps: "Already done in. Sad to say. Savage beasts, the barracuda."

Marc stricken with the pain of the day when Gramps went away.

"Oh, my lovely Gramps. Can you ever forgive me?"

"If you *expunge* the colonial accent, dear boy. Though, does it matter now, except upon the stage of time eternal? For your Shakespearean destiny goes to Gluckenheimer. You, the inheritor of the classic Leadbeater virtues; the personification of the delicious Leadbeater vices; you, of a thousand years of lusty Leadbeaters, the clown prince. Such a one, conceding all to a *Gluckenheimer*."

"I can't bear to look at you, Gramps."

"If the gods who made me perfect can stand the sight, they demand the same of you."

"Please, my lovely Gramps. Put the bandage back on."

"Dear boy, give consideration to the year 2010. You, the toast of London Town. And across the busy little water, the toast of gay Paree. And across the great water, the toast of the Great White Way. And beyond the sunset, if not too damned clever, the toast of the town that reared and raised you. Of such is the destiny that passes to Gluckenheimer."

"I wish you wouldn't do this, Gramps. I've never heard of Gluckenheimer."

"Any more than he has heard of you."

Gramps flexing his fingers and replacing the blindfold.

Marc at once gripped by a terrible pain. Clasping at his chest with opposed hands.

Did one die of heart attacks at sixteen?

Gramps continuing: "Gran at Nemesis, you say? Am I to understand that Gran is the object of this mission? This folly of yours? This expedition that returns you to the scene of the crime and your doom?"

Gramps going on: "Gran appearing at Nemesis? Well, pickle my pelvis. Never a serious intention on her part, my boy. Take my word for it, by noting the magnitude of the diversion she has arranged. Putting our world on the market. A grossness I have sadness in believing of her . . ."

Marc had nothing to say.

"Now, dear boy, do you recall your Gran ever joining us in your jolly play pit when you were four? Or accompanying us to the ocean or the bay? Or to the relevant department of the Geological Museum on that excursion of unhappy memory?

"Pathological fear of sand. As others fear sin. An abhorrence of sand. In her hair. In her shoes. Down her neck. Of insinuating itself into areas not generally discussed. In no way would she be calling my name on the sand, except for sale at maximum going price."

This time was it the spectre that had gone away? Leaving the man?

Gramps said: "To all humans, dear boy, there comes the time to meet the sea-serpent. To some, like me, she comes late. Even then a meeting hastened by my failure to accept the mathematics of seventy-four years. A meeting not seriously intended, I'm told, for I'd have lived another twenty years or so and seen you make your fame. And adorn our family name. Now that cannot be. Control of Destiny not having been entrusted to me."

Marc, unable to protect himself, allowing his hand to pass to Gramps and going out with him into the roaring tides of time.

TWELVE

Leadbeater and
the Seventh Wave

MARC COUNTING seven waves upon the sea. Seven waves like seven avalanches.

A shore and a sea known to him from life and from dreaming.

For round about were the familiar collisions of winds and the seabirds in scores swept into flight paths of blinding speed. And the spray gusting across spuming sands like fine, hard rain.

And there were the two familiar human shapes, if human they ever were, leaning on the wild wind. Making their way down to the high-water mark where the great sea cunningly imitated rest.

Marc thinking: This is how it was on that awful day. I knew the danger then and know it now. Why am I back as if I'd never been away?

You up there. Aren't you going to set me free? You know I'm only sixteen.

The hand of Gramps fixing upon the shoulder of Marc, directing him, propelling him, as always; though in life, in his last year, standing taller than Marc by less than half a head.

Together, walking down the lengthening courses of sand, as if each step forward were but a fraction of a step.

"Yet to some creatures," Gramps said, speaking further of the sea-serpent, "the encounter comes early. Again, it's not for me to say why. Except that by your presence here you've made it easy for those who manage lives."

Gramps and Marc together walking on down the courses of the rivulets rushing to the sea. Marc glancing back to observe the footprints in the sand. The figure of the old one making none.

"This kid in Massachusetts," Gramps said. "Aged sixteen. A considerable 192 centimetres tall. A primary statistic that must interest you, my boy.

"Eyes brown. Hair black. Lips full. Denoting sensuality, I've heard people say, but many a full lip known to me has had little to do with that, other than what is reasonable and required.

"Nose. Of classic form and generous dimension. Allergic to dust, pollen, and sudden changes of wind and temperature. Forever sneezing and wheezing about the place. A trying disability, as you'd know.

"Body: willowy, lean, languid, and rather lovely in a shy, boyish way. In every visible manner appreciably like someone we know.

"And all too often emotional to the point of absurdity. Inviting ridicule and the antics of the mimics. Contributing, in total, towards a picture that must command your fraternal attention, young Marcus Leadbeater, for it could be a picture of you."

Walking on. As if pledged to the sands. As if forever

caught between the last wave and the next. As if seven waves like seven avalanches were to be poised forever offshore.

"This Rudolphus K. Gluckenheimer. Distanced by half a world from you, dear boy. With a father trading from door to door in packets of dubious meat. For pets. God forgive all. And a mother peddling her songs after dark to service her loving commitment to Rudolphus—in surroundings where I'd not care to find a lady of mine. But it's proper that some should fight for the wherewithal and proper that others should have their needs provided. Never has it been otherwise. It's not for us to say why. A significant lady, let me add. A very fine girl."

Coming against the wind, a call.

"Marcus Leadbeater! Is it true I'm being asked again to live it through?"

Gramps and Marc walking on. Each step arduous, tiring, and incomprehensibly short.

"Concerning Rudolphus. Four times weekly attending Miss Gladys Slazenger's Academy of Dramatic Arts in the local Episcopalian Church Hall. Miss Gladys: the second woman of pure gold to figure in the life of this gifted lad. Such is the value of Rudolphus.

"What the devil, some may ask, is Gladys doing in the local Episcopalian Church Hall fooling around with a bunch of kids? All but one, in the context of theatre, not seriously worth the candle? Why not in her rightful place on Broadway or Shaftesbury Avenue? I answer that the Almighty in his wisdom takes care of all. I hope that the pressure of business doesn't lead to his forgetting Gladys in her old age, or I shall have to take steps of my own."

A second call coming against the wind.

"Marcus Leadbeater! I know you hear me. I know you love me in your way. What about some common compassion?"

Said Gramps: "You, young Leadbeater; a thousand years or more of modest privilege in the making. But young Gluckenheimer; through as many seasons of persecution arriving on scene precisely timed to claim your destiny. Marvellous, I say. What say you?"

In Marc's mind the question: "Do you hear me up there? Something screwy's happening down here. If I am what I am, and Rudolphus is what he is, and Gramps knows what he's talking about, how come you can't make room in the world for both of us?"

A third call heard against the wind.

"How many more times will you break my heart? Are you set on leaving me forever? WHY DO YOU IGNORE ME, MARCUS?*"*

Gramps stopping. His locked hand on Marc's shoulder. "Someone called my name!"

"Someone sure did. They've been at it for ages."

"Then for God's sake, why haven't you told me?"

"What's the point when you're not listening. And don't want to. And never will. You've never been different."

"That's cheap and vulgar. I lived by the principle of humane concern for all. Including the struggle not only to consider but to *hear* the views of others. No matter how asinine and indistinct. The latter, notably, in respect to your own."

Marc aggrieved, delivering his judgement. "Talk of humane concern for what others had to say was hard to see while you were alive. And hasn't come easier in the last hour. You're always out to score a point."

"You add absurdity to vulgarity. And no doubt you're about to tell me you didn't know I was deaf."

Marc never finding it easy to keep up with the wiles of the old fox. "You're right. I didn't know you were deaf. It's silly to go on like this. There wouldn't be anyone who'd believe you."

"Then it's a world full of fools."

"It's a world full of people who never knew where they were with you."

"Rubbish."

"Don't rubbish me. I couldn't stand it then and can't stand it now. I don't know why I bother, really I don't. Everybody who loved you came to it in the end. They didn't know why they cared."

Gramps silent.

Seas still roaring like avalanches. Spray still stinging like hard rain. Gulls still hovering, and scattering into arrow lines of flight almost too swift for the eye to track.

Gramps said, "Very well. That's water under the bridge, beyond recall. Now tell me if it's her!"

Marc feeling he'd have liked an apology to the human race. "Your question isn't grammatical."

Gramps, with vehemence: "Answer it."

"I can't. I don't know who *her* is supposed to be."

"Constance!"

"Who's Constance?"

From Gramps a sob. "Even in death . . . These damnable children . . . I can't hear. I can't see. I don't think I can bear it. Trying to feel my way through the universe with nerve ends! *Constance is your grandmother!*"

All right, Marc thought. Constance. When would I have heard of Constance? I thought her name was Bunny.

To Gramps he said, "You've not forgotten, I hope, that I'm a Marcus Leadbeater, too. The lady back there might have no interest in you. You've been dead for months. Not even a body for a burial. Just a plaque on the wall. I've talked myself out of it. Who in the real world would be chasing me?"

Marc looking back.

Twenty or thirty paces back, a girl of marked distinction of about sixteen years. Running fast, but curiously, into the wild onshore wind. And making little headway.

A girl dressed as if for a party. An old-time party. Of the 1940s or 1950s. A flimsy frock brilliantly patterned with triangles, squares, circles, and sums of addition. A frock windblown and wet with sea spray and creased into the kind of figure that aroused Marc's keenest interest. With some modest clearing of the throat. You don't tell your grandfather everything. Any more than he tells you.

The girl seeming to reach out with both hands. But running as if caught on the wrong side of a fast-moving ramp.

"Let me come . . . Let me come . . ."

It wasn't the femme fatale. Much too young. And her hair wasn't gold but a glistening black, and at the distance she dazzled him. Though *dazzled* might not have fairly expressed what he saw or felt.

Gramps, the man with the Midas touch. If he'd played the ponies he'd have made a fortune . . .

Friends, Romans, countrymen. Allow me to voice your appreciation and mine of this captivating creature. A world full of them and all out of reach. Denied to thee and me, for nothing like it was meant for us.

"A girl," Marc reported to the grandparent, "like daylight after a dreadful night. Hence, with sorrow, I report that never have I set eyes on the like of it. And with deeper

sorrow add that her sights must be set on you. Though
much too young for you, old spook. Too young even for
the most improper blessings of our holy father Leadbeater
upon the mountain. I believe she considers herself to be in
pursuit of you. Some might think it's cute. The police might
think it invites investigation. How come you've kept out
of gaol?"

Gramps, in the same moment, remote, pointer in left
hand, standing before a blackboard as wide as a room.

Marc, one of a thousand or more, all of indefinite age,
up near the ceiling on a seat as hard as a park bench,
notebook and ballpoint at the ready, stretching the eyes,
hearing, and understanding, for it was a vanity of this man
never to write in a large hand, never to use a microphone,
never to weaken a serious thought with simplicity.

"It's the mathematics," Gramps was saying. "A weight
too great for the common herd. I have no quarrel with the
common herd while they keep their distance.

"In mathematics, we approach the outskirts of God's
language. Let the common herd be warned. God makes
himself known through conundrums. And problems. And
equations. And ultimately through elegant solutions.

"What use could God have for words? For vocalizations
of animal origin converted to wriggles and scribbles and
scratches and scrapes? Interminably dragging their way
across the centuries? Rooted in the human capacity, inex-
haustibly, to vary the shape of the grunt.

"Would you have God confine himself to animal or mechanical forms? Like an educated conscript under the command of a boorish NCO?

"A single thought originating in the God-mind exceeds
the sum of human knowledge. Now God being love, what
enlightened creature would fail to move heaven and earth

to express creature love in the language most approximating that of God, the original, the total mathematician? What else can love be but the perfect equation?"

Upon the blackboard, Gramps writing rapidly. Faintly, the squeal of a stub of chalk. Thirteen symbols. Sixty-eight centimetres from left to right. From the distance impossible to read.

Gramps stepping aside.

"Behold what I believe, in humility, to be the sum of love. I append this equation to the Holy Ten of Mosaic fame. And give you the Twelfth Commandment. Written as it was given to me. The Eleventh you should know by instinct, and woe betide you if you don't.

"Forty-two years I lived with my love. This is my declaration in honour of her, my equal, whom I, once a man of thirty-two, carried off. Tucked, in a manner of speaking, under my strong right arm. She being sixteen."

Was it simply another step aside that he took? For instantly all was gone, and everything to do with order, words, mathematics, and love was gone with him.

Everywhere the world had become bruising and roaring and violent and once more believable. For what else could the mighty sea be where it met the rocks of the shore but roaring and believable?

Marc's body beaten from its blows past numbering.

Please, please, get me out of here!

All this talk of God. And of love. A ruse to get me off guard and carry me into the sea. Under his strong left arm. I, too, being sixteen. I, under one arm. This Constance, under the other.

So then Marc thought: We're with the sharks now, and the barracuda, and him. We'll all be wearing bandages

where our heads used to be. So he's won again. Did he
ever lose?

Gran, are you there?

Are you really such a sexy young girl? Don't you know
you're going to be the mother of my father? Who's *such* a
straight guy. Don't you know you'll be the grandmother of
me, who gets embarrassed over nothing at all? Him heaven
knows how old and you still sixteen?

Please, somebody, get me out of here.

THIRTEEN

Leadbeater's Shakespearean Touch

THE VOYAGER'S return . . .

Was a smell entering Marc's world? A smell as welcome as that of dry land when continents were as far apart as planets?

Was he climbing a last ladder through a lightening dark towards a call from the mast: *"Land ahoy"*?

Was a way home to be found, after all? And best of all, had he lived long enough to find it?

> *Hold me tight that I may weep,*
> *Safe from the journeys of sleep.*

On the air, an entrancing trace of Rose Geranium, his very favourite soap.

Source of the aroma not to be seen, for his eyelids wouldn't part.

"Wake up, Marc . . ."

A soft voice out there instead of avalanches. A human presence, warm and close, instead of shades, instead of

ghosts. Hands to his shoulders. The electric touch of Rose
Geranium. The electric charge of shocking pink.

> *Leave me never,*
> *Hold me ever.*

"Come on, Marc."

"I'm hearing you, ma'am."

"Then let's have you out of there."

"Out of where?"

"That's for you to tell."

Not this time, lady. That's a secret until failing memory
blots it out.

Marc then resuming, even languidly, the wilder aspects
of his waking fantasy by granting it the pleasure of a last
canter around the paddock. Just knowing that he lay upon
the famous bed of the infamous femme fatale. Which would
put him in a scene as lush as clover and set him about with
the reds and blacks and satins of sin. A scene as blissful,
my friends, as the misty encounters of the dog-tired hours
a fellow can never quite recall, nor ever quite forget.

Reaching, at last, an upright position. Aided by the
hands of the lady. Swallowing against a sudden unmanly
swelling of the throat and gut. Marc not deliriously excited
by the acid taste of the swelling, reducing him to no fit
condition for taking a sight of the land lying out there
beyond the closed eyelids.

Nothing functional to see with, anyway.

Eyes leaden. Lids leaden. Head leaden. Leadenness in
almost every part of him. A Leadbeater for trailing with
the barracuda bait.

Marc therefore content to swoon into the lady's arms.

Arms being available, one avails!

While everywhere about now breathed the breath of country gardens perfumed with drifts of Rose Geranium. And of secret sighs in scented arbours. And of other confidential matters whispered where sweet alyssum grew about the knuckled feet of sundials that never breathed a word of it to each other.

An unusually hoarse clearing of the Baskerville throat.

Oh man. Give me the wobbles. Give me the frails. And the permanent incapacity to enjoy them like this.

I have come home to where the heart is.

"I'm right with you, ma'am."

Leaning where it's soft.

Leaning where it's firm.

Leaning where the fellow may take comfort from the reality of flesh and blood. Though where he may become aware of the spirit. Where he may draw closer to the ancient meeting places of fantasy and life. The trysting places. The rendezvous. *Rendezvous*, in this context, not to be considered singular. Hence, perhaps, the rendezvousouses?

Oh, this softly literate mood and the lush joys of language.

Down with barbarism. Down with emphatically sainted grandparents and their mathematical formulae!

What can language be but love? Which cuts that old spook off in the middle of his arithmetical prime!

Language and love, Marc thinking, in this instance being related to the aesthetic consideration. To those aspects of love concerned wholly with the values of the spirit.

Mark further thinking: I quote, for example, the pristine pure appreciation of the beauty of the human form felt by a majority of healthy young fellows in the presence of ladies of elegant texture. The flesh-pink duchess in the work by Goya coming to mind. As no doubt she had a habit of coming to the mind of Goya. Or he'd have painted her in jeans with pimples.

Oh, hear me, all ye suffering youth. All ye who are deprived. All ye who, consumed by impatience, must continue to wait upon time.

All ye need is a year or more and a dash of good old-fashioned good luck. Such as being in the right place at the right moment. Such as assorted young gentlemen and privileged elders (I'm compelled to assume) have enjoyed from time to time.

Then, beneath thy hurting head must lie the sweet cushion God provides for the sorrows and trials of humankind.

Marc thinking even further: Oh, what exquisite material. I'd claim it if I could be sure it was mine.

I'd copyright it. I'd market it. I'd print it on tea towels with appropriate illustration. And on offensively bottle-green bathmats. I'd make my fortune in street stalls on Easter Saturday mornings.

Who needs scripts by W. Shakespeare upon which to sustain one's brilliant career? Though I'll bet W. Shakespeare got to my sweet cushion before I did. Like he seems to have got everywhere else. Either him or Solomon singing his song to his pretty little pomegranates.

Between these two fellows, what's left relating to the femme that they didn't think of first?

Where was the Unfair Practices Committee of the Playwrights Union? Who paid 'em the hush money? How come they didn't march on Stratford-upon-Avon? Or Solomon's Temple?

It's a sobering experience confronting the *Dictionary of Quotations*. When I grow up I'm drafting a new one with thirty pages drawn from Leadbeater.

In the meantime, I know where I'm leanin'. Do I ever

just. The safe harbour at the end of all voyages. The cure
for all complaints. For toothache. For the broken leg. For
unprincipled cultural gluts on the literary love market.

"Marc."

Marc being most handsomely supported, thank you, and
voting for continuing communion with these here rarefied
pleasures of the spirit. Electing not to resort to the risk of
peeping at the living world beyond the leaden eyelids, for
reality might spoil the heaven of modest proportions created
within.

"Are you all right, Marc?"

"Oh, ma'am. Like the perennial pea in the pod."

"I mean, Marc, *all right!*"

The tone of voice, the possibility of an underlying cen-
sure, bringing to mind Miss Gorgeous at critical moments
in the classroom. Compelling him to make extra deeply
seated clearing sounds of the throat. A concession to up-
bringing, dated circa 1930, though not initiated in regard
to his own person until a half century later. And, further,
to the dignity of this here present accomplished female, this
perfumed personage, this *participant* in the cunning de-
ceptions of Sadie the Scented Lady. (Mental note in the
Future's Book: *Sadie. Worth at least a cultural visit un-
accompanied by the delectable Rosemary.*)

Marc with a large breath saying, " 'All right' expresses
it, ma'am. All things considered. Being back where people
are composed of the visible elements. I'm all for these here
elements, running real hot."

"I'm to suppose you've returned from where the status
quo was not?"

Big sigh.

"You'd never believe, ma'am. Honest you wouldn't."

"Try me."

"Recent adventures are not for repeat viewing until the little kids are in bed. And parents are sound asleep and removed from the contaminated area. Real harrowing. Enough to make you swear off toasted cheese at suppertime. What was it that put me there?"

"The Chardonnay."

"Oh no. Not instant repartee. Not off the top of the head. Not without serious consideration of the hundreds of preferred alternatives."

"The *Chardonnay*."

"To come again, ma'am, italicizing it, so to speak, can only be termed ill motivated. An act typical of routine adult insensitivity. Coming from where I would've been expecting a less restrictive frame of mind."

"The Chardonnay, young man. Insufficiently diluted to meet the limitations of what the medical profession, in a lighter moment, might call your constitution."

"You're cutting close to the bone, lady. I warn you of the dangers of outraging the dignity of Leadbeaters."

"I stand warned and regret that you have fallen short of your expectations. And add that you may well be denied the ultimate achievement of skating down skid row. I need to acquaint you with the metabololic fact—"

"Lady! Could it be something other than Rose Geranium I'm smelling round here? Have you been finishing off the Chardonnay?"

"I continue—the adjectivial fact that you're not constructed to handle a bottle a day. Most of us aren't. At present I doubt if you're constructed to handle an ice-cold lemonade. Which leaves me troubled that I've failed to entertain you responsibly. Unless it was that you came to me already half sloshed."

"Are you *inferring* that I'm a lush?"

"Young man, concerning the unknown pasts and futures of this day, I assume you lapsed into your coma at the brink of telling me. I also assume that your coma did not pass without event."

Marc giving consideration to these various traps set for the young player. "It was," he said, "a deadly dream."

"I believe it. I couldn't allow it to go on."

Marc considering that also. "Are you saying I didn't finish it? I'll die if it's going to be a family saga of twenty-six episodes. I'll never risk going to sleep again."

"Important dreams, I understand, say what they have to say, even when worried spectators cut them short. But taking them literally may not be wise."

Marc trying hard to open his eyes. Believing it to be long past time. But not able to make it happen.

"Would you call your dream important, Marc?"

"That's a terrible question to put to me in my present state of ill health. *Of course it was important.*"

"Would you call it a recurring dream?"

"I hope you're not suggesting it might be."

"Then I'm asking you to write it down before you lose it."

"If I had my way, I'd lose it all right; I'd give it away. With a block of chocolate and a year of cut lawns thrown in free."

"I'll get pen and paper."

"You won't."

"It's the cardinal rule."

"Not my rule. Not my cardinal."

Upon the lady, a faintly wounded expression.

"Happily condemned to death was his loving way of putting it. The two of us enjoying the hearty breakfast that precedes the hilarious execution! Breakfast getting served

up to *him* by the bucket. Nothin' coming my way except
the promise. Same as always."

Marc brooding.

His jaw jutting.

"The things he said about my life . . ."

"Marc . . . It was not your Gramps. It was a *dream.*
And may require explanation."

"My destiny, Gramps said, was going to some other kid.
There he was: chopping my life off in my own hearing.
Handing it over to this other kid. Rudolph! Rudolphus!
Glockenspiel or Blickenhammer. Does it matter?"

"I'll have no idea until you tell me."

"Do you keep a clock? What time is it? My sainted grandparent marching me into the surf by the scruff this very
day to meet the sea-serpent. The scene being Nemesis. As
he said was set up in the first place, but I wouldn't play.
The outcome, he said, today, would be mathematically
clean, tidy, and total. Or something like that.

"Gran was there. Aged sixteen.

"Give thought, lady, to coming face to face with your
grandmother aged sixteen. Like being around before you're
born. Same as *you* might feel stumbling onto your grandfather aged sixteen strutting about the place trying to excite
the girls.

"Did Gramps ever tell you he carried her off aged sixteen? All filmy and feminine and enough to drive you
frantic.

"A real crisis coming to know that this vision is your
grandmother. Looking like a copy of vintage Miss Gorgeous. If that's how she presented her credentials, no wonder Gramps flipped. Him being the professional bachelor
of a mere thirty summers or so.

"So now we've got Gran, post-mortem, pleading with

him to take her into the sea. As if getting drowned was the real big deal.

"While offshore—like they'd been painted into a picture—we've got these seven waves. All the time roaring. All the time breaking. Like seven permanent avalanches.

"He had bandages hiding his face. And listened at hardly any time. Talked over me. Like he had a habit of doing when he was feeling playful. Or ornery."

"Don't be unjust, Marc."

"This time saying as well as not seeing me, he wasn't hearing me either. Telling me he'd been deaf all my life. Was that the thing for him to say?"

"For all you appear to know, it could have been."

"Lady . . . This is my oration . . . I'm not looking for responses . . .

"This kid Blickenwicker. His mum singing in shady dives wearin' a G-string. His dad sellin' globs of meat in little packets from door to door. All this humiliation so Blockenwacker can be the great actor instead of me. So Wockenblacker can live my life instead of me. Who the hell am I, anyway? And who the hell is Wickenblacker? There I was tellin' the gods the world was big enough for both of us, but gettin' the brush-off.

"Do you dream real lousy dreams like that? Like they know things you don't know. If mine's recurring, I'll be taking a hammer when I go to bed and hitting me on the head every time it shows.

"It was a haunting. Like I had at his front door before I came pounding round here. Real unwholesome. I've got a persecution in pursuit. Along with grandmothers and scheming little graspers like Miss Hudd and Sons. What's happened to my Gramps? That he'd allow this to happen to me?

"Who is it that's being unjust? You used the word, lady. Did I ask for an inheritance? All I wanted was my Gramps the way I knew him. Now, if I've got anything, it's the right to ask why he set it up so it could happen.

"All those years we were great mates. Why's he left me a terrible mess? How *could* the feeling we had be part of a big act? He left me his house, didn't he? To care for and remember him by. Which everyone knows I'd have honoured to the letter, although they're into me about it now. They all hate me now, because it's come to me instead of them. Even people who are supposed to love me.

"But how much is that little grasper, Miss H. and Sons, saying my house will cost me? She won't tell. Have a guess. Three hundred thousand? Four hundred thousand? It's the crummiest inheritance I've ever heard of. I'll be paying it off till I die.

"I broke two toes helping my Gramps with the floors. I got a rusty nail through one foot and everyone thought I'd die of tetanus. I went through the ceiling with a bag of galvanized clouts and was left swinging by my chin. Lucky I didn't hang. I cracked three ribs falling off the ladder when we were doing the TV. Tore my shoulder muscle off the bone planting four of his bloody trees. Digging the holes when I was six, and hardly able to lift an arm for six months afterwards. Couldn't hold a pencil. Had to do everything in my head. All the kids writing out their names and rushing home to show their mums and me not able to make a scratch. Still can't hold a mean tennis racquet. You should see me, poking about the court like an old duck."

Marc lying there, eyes shut. Just lying there, supported by the Shakespearean touch.

Shortly, softly, she said, "Well, perhaps now you're ready for tea?"

FOURTEEN

Leadbeater's
Low-Fat Diet

TEA?

What happened to lunch?

"Whose tea? What tea?"

"The lunch on our plates. The *Low-Fat Food for Your Good Health*. So we come to a moment of truth. Does it stand the warming over without turning into soup?"

Marc not up with the change of topic. "It can't be time for tea. You're having me on."

"Dear friend, it's 5:01."

A day distinguised by firsts.

Of epoch-making events.

And no lunch.

And of the first small, great step on the ladder to fame. The *dear friend* of a scarlet woman and not yet out of Year Eleven! Let this be known, far and wide, and even the Year Twelve freaks will be queueing to kiss my foot at a dollar a time.

Marc sufficiently moved to open fractionally one eye.

"Did I hear myself, ma'am, referred to as your dear friend?"

In the soft light, there she was.

Man. Looking like the picture on the cover of an inspirational book for those suffering from too much emotional involvement.

Old enough to be second cousin Philippa. Old enough to be Auntie Brenda O'Reilly. But leaving both characters clear out of sight. Looking like why Gramps came knocking at her door after whatever it was that had happened at home with Gran in the forty years between. But all judgements relating to ladies being highly suspect and highly subjective—a Grampsian statement without a doubt.

5:01?

Dreams, people reckoned, were over in moments.

Time had come for someone to recalculate the duration of the moment. Someone like Gramps. With lots of eternity to spare.

Said the femme fatale, "I see myself as your comrade. Yes, and your dear friend. Whatever you wish me to be, I'll try to be, in moderation."

Oh, a lady delectable in the sense of the ever-delectable Rosemary. Gorgeous, in the style of the gorgeous Miss G., without the sting of Miss G. And even if the soft cushion of Marc's trials and sorrows were less Shakespearean than he had hoped, and even if he were not reclining upon the famous bed of alleged ill repute, it was, at least, an encounter close enough to support his bedtime fantasies for a year or two, glazed eyes projecting images onto the ceiling.

"How," he asked, "did I get back to this here sinking red settee?"

"We managed it together, after a fashion."

"What sort of fashion?"

"The imagining I leave to you."

"You've got to be teasing, ma'am. I couldn't be three sheets to the wind on fizzy lemonade."

"Would I tease my dear friend whose fortunes I've followed since the famous ninth-birthday affair aboard the Queenscliff ferry."

After a stunned pause: "You *couldn't* have been there."

"To the contrary. And not entirely by coincidence. Travelling at the same time, shall we say? Any honest girl with a crush on her professor would understand. As for you, you mini-monster, too much chocolate. Too much coconut. Too much gluttony."

"That's not fair, ma'am. This is how rumours start. This is how reputations are ruined. It was my *tenth* birthday. And my illness was due to the heavy swell and a paltry three little somethings called strawberry ice cream spiders. To this day the sight of a strawberry or the smell of one . . ."

"Next question, Marc . . . About his being deaf. You weren't serious?"

"All my questions are serious. How do you think I get educated?"

"You must know he was hard-of-hearing."

Marc's eyes becoming round. "Of course he wasn't hard-of-hearing. Did he pull that act on you, too? He's the one they should've put on the stage."

"He lip-read."

"Oh, come on . . . Across crowded rooms? Out of the back of his head? He heard face to face or around the corner like a hotted-up listening machine?"

"How could you not know that year by year he heard less and less?"

"Knowing's got nothing to do with it."

"Why would I deceive you?"

"It's a lost cause, lady. I'm not buying it. You've been telling me my dreams are not psychic."

"He was deaf. But uncommonly adept at concealing it, for reasons I'll not even guess at. Knowing him as I knew him."

"Then you knew him better than I did. And better than my dad. And better than my Gran. She spent half her life yelling after him."

"So I'm told."

"Lady, that's rude. He was famous for not taking notice of anybody."

"There, in a word, you have it."

"No, I don't have it! Famous for walking round in the big dream reflecting on the theory of relativity or whatever he'd decided to rubbish for that week."

"It dates back to an old injury, Marc. To do with jumping from a second-floor window."

"I know about the students and the wastepaper basket. I know about the fire and the second-floor window. If you tell me you were one of the students, I'll hit you with this red settee."

"Can you work an IBM keyboard?"

"No."

"I don't accept that. You'd have learnt in primary school."

"Lady, it's not that I look like a twit. I am a twit. I'm the consolation of my dull-witted peers and the despair of my betters."

"You've had an important dream."

"A very wearin' one."

"And you've dreamt it under my roof, which gives me a proprietary interest. From what I've already heard, I regret that serious note must be taken of it."

"Serious note of it is what I've been taking!"

"Then you'll understand how highly I'd value a firsthand written record. If you can't use the computer keyboard, for any reason, like crass stupidity, I'll give you a microphone."

"Oh, ma'am . . ."

"As a special favour. As from time to time I glance in from the kitchen reconstituting our expensive little lunch, let me be among the first to observe the young Leadbeater fulfilling his destiny."

"I'm not with you, ma'am."

"Of course you are. The keyboard? Or the microphone?"

"Oh, come on. You know what this'll do to the expectations of my family. Even to a few of my own. If I go for the keyboard, every Leadbeater, living or dead, will throw a fit."

"You could be a writer."

"Ma'am. *Please!* The Leadbeater fits will be made of bricks, all thrown at my head. We'll have crummy old spooks and aircraft captains shrieking all over the place. *Don't tell us this kid reckons on starving in a garret for twenty years while he's learning how to spell. We thought we had an Olivier. A Barrymore. A Gielgud. A real big-time, bright-light Shakespearean strutter-up-and-down. The first such Leadbeater since 1812. About to reflect glory on all around. We've spent a fortune training him up to it since he was eight.* Just you wait and see. I've heard it all before."

"You could be another David Garrick."

"Who's he?"

"Marc . . ."

"Oh hell . . . Give me the keyboard, then. And every word over two syllables, watch me spell it wrong."

Suddenly she said, "Second thoughts. Your dream."

A great gravity was coming upon her.

"Your Gran . . ."

"Ma'am. No!"

"Her life could be an issue more pressing than our tea."

"Nothing in this world's more pressin' than our tea. I've got a hole in me like a mine shaft."

"Your grandmother's need may be greater."

"Hardly ever eats a thing, ma'am. Pecks at her food like a bird. Her need relating to me is like her need of a ten-course Chinese banquet. My Gran having demonstrated today her magnificent disinterest. You wouldn't know the half of it!"

"Then enlighten me!"

"There's nothin' I could tell without grievous loss of face."

"Tell me what there is!"

"Look, lady, you're provoking unneeded crises. My Gran didn't show. A sleight-of-hand act. A trick of the phone. The only way I can talk to her is over the wire."

Marc with a hand as if about to clap it to his head. "She's got more faces than the India-rubber man at the Royal Show."

"Yes?"

"Got her phone wired up to some secret address from where she's directing the forces of confusion. Like selling everything that's mine. Like making out to all and sundry she's still living there eagerly anticipating my imminent arrival."

"Did she *anticipate* your arrival? Or did you drop in like a bolt from heaven?"

"I'm not playin' games, ma'am. From prehistoric times it was set for three-thirty today. But from her very mouth, within the confines of this very town, she blurts into my ear today that it's tomorrow. Hornblowers! She thought she had everything set up for me to arrive *after* the auction. I'd have walked into a SOLD sign pasted over the front fence and dropped dead in the middle of the street. If you'd been passing then, instead of when you did, you'd have squashed me flat. Me mum would've scratched your eyes out. Me dad would've sued you. And me Gran would've sent you a letter of thanks."

"So you came today, instead of tomorrow, and early as well?"

Marc getting a creepy feeling. "Don't start accusing me, ma'am. I don't feel like pickin' up the blame. My mum knew nothing about the auction either or she'd have told me. That's one lady I can trust. I came down here to take my Gran to all the places I'd ever gone with Gramps. Though I'd been looking forward to it like I was coming down here to me execution."

"You can trust me, too, Marc. But I believe we should call on your Gran."

"You've got a death wish. She'll come at you with a machine gun. Meanwhile, I'm *starvin'*."

"Regard it as training for life."

"Didn't even get fed in my dream! Even my spirit is starvin'! Me spectre's gone all pale and pasty."

"The fate of half the writers I know."

Marc taking a deep breath. "I had breakfast this morning at 7:00. And now you say it's 5:01."

"It was 5:01 fifteen minutes ago. But I had no breakfast of any kind."

"That was because of your figure. Me mum's the same. And my kid sisters. You should see their figures! Tweedledeeski and Tweedledumski. Despite going without breakfast."

"We're on our way, Marc. Calling on your Gran."

Deep within Marc, a sigh.

"I'll faint," he said. "You'll have to hold me up. You'll have to carry me over your shoulder."

She presented a firm hand and pulled him to his feet, but in the same movement spun him into contact with herself. He found her arms about him and her head against his chest.

Heaven help us, Marc said to himself.

Then, further: Heaven help me in particular. Lovely lady, you're all around me like a fog. But I told you I'm a puff of woof. I dissolve under pressure. Like raspberries. I'd be a shockin' disappointment. Ask Rosemary. Along with other patient friends who ought to remain nameless, but I'm thinking of Heather and Fiona and Ruthie and Josie and my poor cousin Eleanor, who really has put her heart and soul into it. It's a breeze for you femmes, comparatively speaking. You can be steaming like kettles and still present respectable fronts. But you'd know all that, ma'am. Being thirty or more. Along with being infamous.

Marc, fortunately, remaining wise enough to address only himself, which brought him to the end of the embrace.

So on we go, he thought, along life's busy way. Living to the full the life of the lost opportunity. Now, what are these big baby-blue eyes of hers doing full of big wet tears?

Lady, you'll ruin your makeup. All to no good end. All you've done is join the club. Along with all the femmes of my acquaintance who've tried the close approach.

They call me Snow-clad Silver Czar. Woof. Much to me embarrassment. As he who loves 'em all, but washes up whiter than your favourite Samoyed. And retires each night to his virtuous couch with his little woolly blanket and his illustrated book of fairy tales.

"Dear Marc. We must go."

How come this lady doesn't reach my collarbone? I've been thinking of her as a strapping great Valkyrie. Like the physiotherapist with the prominent eyes and the flaxen plaits who works on my frozen shoulder, rolling up her sleeves, licking at her lips, showing her chiselled teeth.

The femme said, "You know it's waiting for you. But today, at least, you won't be facing it alone."

Marc giving birth to the panics he'd been trying to suppress.

"The telephone," she said, "is all yours. Tell her you're about to visit."

After a pause for breath and recuperation, he said, "I told her that this morning. And when I got there, in half a minute flat, she wasn't to be found."

"Tell her again."

"She doesn't live there."

"Confirm it. Call the number."

"She's moved and taken the number with her."

"Possibly. But the phone may ring at both addresses."

"Oh, lady, out in the big wide world I'll never stand a chance."

Marc dialling the number. Feeling as if he needed a week in bed on his own. Feeling as if he were exposing himself to the infection of violence by death. Dialling the magic number that used to bring Gramps to the line but now connected him to some secret society speaking with the voice of Gran.

"She's not answering."

"Give her a chance."

"She's not answering! I know how long it takes her to get there. I've been dialling this number all my life."

"Very well. We'll take the car."

FIFTEEN

Here Comes
Marcus Leadbeater XVI

MARC SURE of nothing. As if tangles and knots of fright were cross-wiring his feelings and short-circuiting his head. But an honoured principle of Grampsian times came lurching into view: *Leadbeater men treat ladies as ladies, particularly when the panic's on.*

A wise one was our Gramps . . .

Marc making a leap at each door in turn and opening it with a sweep for the femme to pass through. Then slamming it after her. And heading on her heels for the car, just short of the run, heart thudding, stomach perilously close to the turning edge. Reaching out around her and opening up the car and shutting her in and striding round to the passenger side, thinking, All is not lost. The blood of the hero runs fast. Here comes Marcus Leadbeater XVI. Though upon reflection, was it not Louis XVI who had lost his head?

The inside lock barring Marc's entry.

Marc tapping politely on the glass.

The lady concentrating upon banging her knuckles on the instrument dials.

Marc thumping on the roof.

"You in there. Lemme in."

Marc receiving his reward and proceeding in the short term to ram both kneecaps into the bottom rim of the dash and his head into the roof.

Some stupid little hobbit. Some gnome. Having cranked the seat forward to the limit of its run. In Paradise may he/she be taller than a tree and be stuffed lengthwise down a rabbit hole!

The lady now fiercely committed to the top rim of the dash, banging at it with the heel of her hand.

There were people Marc knew who encouraged their cars with poetry readings. Others hit them with hammers. When, in some future life, he got his hands on the noble Jaguar with its twin exhausts and elegant chrome, he'd be stroking it with feathers.

Gramps is dead!

Carry it with you. Write it in red.

Tell yourself, mate, with the femme at your side there'll be nothing in the house to maim you.

The Gramps of this day being no connection, the expert says, with the Gramps of real life or the Gramps of real death.

The expert being the doctor of dreams. The physician of fantasies.

The landscape outside not changing as anticipated.

The physician looking brittle, now fiercely shaking the wheel with both hands, perhaps to dislodge the steering lock . . .

Marc further addressing himself: Who knows better than

me that the old blighter's dead? Who else did the yelling and the swimmin' after? Who else got dumped in the shockin' sea? Stirring up the agony in my shoulder got when I was six from planting his Sydney bloody blue gum and his scarlet bloody oak. Gramps, historically, taking the contrary view:

"Dear boy. Your recollection is unmathematical. They were but little baby trees in four-inch pots. Still on mother's milk. You were poking them into sand. Not blasting them into rock. You tore your shoulder on the merry-go-round, in infantile rage because the prancing horse wouldn't buck."

"Ma'am! What you doing there? Shaking a cocktail?"

The femme's brow bristling. *"The key won't turn. The car won't start."*

"If my dad's jumbo won't start, he tries the front-door key. The back-door key. The key to the post office box. Then the crew empty their pockets. And the passengers empty their pockets. You've never seen so many keys in your life."

The femme flashing him a glare, wrenching the offending artifact from the dash, and registering shock.

"That had no business even fitting the lock!"

Snatching at her purse and upending it in her lap.

Marc allowing himself a few moments of satisfaction before sliding back into the anguish of his expectations. These looking like the underwater horrors lurking in the bookshelves of the great man's study. The Arthur Rackham drawings for Wagner's *Ring.* The only light relief between the covers being the three young ladies swimming hither and thither with their clothes off. Not that Nemesis in present circumstances held out much hope of that.

The car. Now jolting. And lurching. In peril of reversing at irreversible speed into the hedge of *Enormicus japonicus*. A kind of agonizing black-and-white comedy.

Marc: "Oh my goodness."

Plunging tail-first across the gutter into the street.

A scream of brakes and a scream of abuse.

Marc turning quite pale.

The femme recovering with a quick lick of her dry lips and a charge for the corner. Taking it like a runaway. Charging for the next corner. Taking it like someone under the influence. The panorama ahead juddering into view like a family picture in the Christmas-night slide show.

The street of childhood holidays. Of funerals. Of crowds in mourning served by caterers with sandwiches and Sauternes. Of Forsythes. Of hauntings. Of hoardings as big as Ping-Pong tables. This one having now acquired a broad band across its face:

TOMORROW 11 A.M. THIS STUNNING EDWARDIAN
WILL YOU BE THE ONE?

Miss Hudd and Sons. You're the bottom of the pit.

The Forsythe sisters at their front gate. Adding further richness to the scene. Supported by the local cheer squad. Rehearsing, perhaps, preliminary rites of adoration for enactment before the big-time cash buyer about to come on stage.

"Oh, sire. Bless thy humble servants with the smile of thy presence. Thy pet cobras we'll feed whilst thou art absent among kings and princes. And we'll direct missiles of discreetness at the filthy pigeons if they alight upon thy roof for disgusting purposes."

Now vehicles. Lined up in Indian file along the kerb.

Seen in the same glance that took in the blur of past and
present and conjecture and the Christmas-night slide show.

Among the vehicles, a police car looking like tomorrow's
headlines. The other vehicles looking like seven plain-
clothed vehicles for plain-clothes cops.

Marc, in the instant, knowing all.

"She's hung herself."

A moment, like the moment at Nemesis, when the head
of Gramps failed to show.

"Or shot herself, or something."

A hand coming to his shoulder.

"We should've burned the rope and smashed the guns
and taken away the poisons. You can't think of everything,
can you? Oh, drive straight in. I shouldn't have drunk that
stuff. I shouldn't have gone to sleep. Oh, God, what have
I done by being at your place?"

The femme letting rip!

"Nothing. Nothing! At sixteen years of age the Almighty
does not require you to carry the world on your back."

Coming to a rough-and-ready stop in the middle of the
entry.

A sandwich board like the flat hand of a policeman:

PEDESTRIAN ACCESS ONLY

FINAL INSPECTION

5:30 TO 8 P.M. TODAY

HUDD AND SONS

ALWAYS SERVING YOU

Marc's head toppling forward as if it had become an
unbearable weight. Then letting go of all breath; the old
fog of incredulity and incompetence rising up to fill him
instead.

His eyes seeking the lady.

"My Gran's crazy. What would she have done with me tomorrow, or today? Or at any time at all?"

"Marc, I don't think I know. I'm wondering if she ever knew herself."

"These police. Do they reckon on turning it into a cop shop? Are they in there measuring it up for cells?"

The femme backing off from the entry.

Marc wrenching at his seat belt. "I'm gettin' in there. I'm goin' through 'em! I've had enough."

"I forbid it."

"Is it my house or isn't it?"

Marc swinging open the door.

"I forbade it!"

The obligatory brakes screaming on the bitumen nearby.

Marc for the merest moment subsiding. Was this dame *ever* going to move a metre or a mile without putting some poor beggar up a tree?

Her available hand, in the same moment, having fastened on a fistful of his hair.

"Let go of me!"

"You're a rampant reflex! You'll kill us both."

"If I don't, you will. Let go o' my hair!"

The femme, one-handed, reaching a parking space three house blocks farther on.

"I want a promise that you won't move!"

"Bananas!"

"I can't park with one hand."

"You couldn't park with two hands. I've got a mum who drives like Piquet. You drive like a clown on a one-wheel bike."

The femme stoically aligning herself with the kerb and scarcely a metre from it.

"The place is crawling with cops, lady. They'll have you for parking in the middle of the street."

"They know me."

"I'll bet they do."

"When you promise to behave, I'll let go of your hair."

"I promise or you'll make me bald!"

"Then you may get out. But you may not run. Or I'll bring you down."

"You and whose football team?"

"Despite all, you're my very special friend, Marc Leadbeater. Give thought to that. And give thought to the morrow. I abhor the idea of a hooligan running loose past the Forsythes. Or running loose in the house. I urge you not to bring dishonour upon yourself, your family, or me. I'm in enough trouble. Aren't you?"

Marc waiting on the pavement, presenting a long, lean, and impassive back to the Forsythes.

"Good lad. Now remember, no matter what we find in here, a million ways lie open for you to botch it. When you feel the urge to express an opinion, bite the lip, even if you bleed all over your collar."

"Maybe we should just skip it, ma'am. What about your place instead? For our nice quiet tea?"

No comment from the lady.

Marc walking on her gutter side (treating ladies as ladies when the panic's on), matching her pace.

The Forsythes and the cheering squad looming up.

Oh, you powers up there! Mercy. Is it possible to ease me painlessly off this hook?

In answer to the plea, Marc rising above himself and looking down.

Oh, ecstacy. Oh, blissful detachment. Ain't rigid self-control a joyous state o' mind!

Down there, Marc observing the lanky kid and the lovely lady compelled to walk wide around the Forsythes and the unbending orbit of the cheer squad. An aggregation sometimes addressed as the Smut Society. Occupying the full breadth of pavement and conceding none of it.

"Dr. Campbell. And young Marcus Leadbeater." The silken voice behind the ivory smile of Miss Fidelia. In the very best Home County tradition. "You've found each other. How charming . . ."

The femme, striding on, allowing her reply to drop behind: "Good evening, neighbours . . ."

Marc, from on high, thus watching the fellow below and his lady protector turning through the gateway, skirting the deplorable sandwich board, confronting the path to the haunted doorstep, and pausing for several moments as if by arrangement.

Here we are, then, Marc Leadbeater and the femme fatale. At the brink of the brink. *Having found each other. How charming.* A thrust from the demented magpie that wounds less than intended.

But am I forty? Am I greying at the temples? If I were, ma'am, we'd set the world on fire. Then all we'd need would be long life to bask in the glow of the coals.

Marc watching their progress, step following step, along the cobbled path laid by Gramps.

Gran up there ahead. Gran in there safe and sound. Oh, please. How could I face that lousy beach again?

Cobblestones for this path gathered by the sainted grandparent and the faithful minion from creek beds, rock pools, and roadsides. Carried home in plastic bags, pockets, and picnic baskets. ("Keeping it private, my champion of the big mouth. Or the greenies'll have our guts. But I reckon the universe owes us the loan of a few pebbles. When we're gone, they can scratch 'em out and hurl 'em at our tomb-stones.")

Marc coming down into himself with a thud.

The front door looking more or less as he'd left it. Stand-ing wide. Under guard of the magic Garuda bird. Rein-forced by the monumental absence. Or the monumental presence. As the case may have been.

Marc holding back.

"Come along."

"He was here, ma'am. He gave me the push. He might as well have spoken it out loud."

"In the light of what's followed, can you be surprised? Torn between his love of her and his love of you. In his shoes, clanking his chains, I'd have done the same."

In a whisper: "Lady, I can do without your rough-hewn homespuns."

"That'll do. That'll do."

The femme: with ears on stalks like his own.

Several persons in conversation more or less visible sev-eral steps into the gloom of the entry.

Marc raising his voice to a hiss: "They'd better not be cops!"

The femme hissing back, "Disrespect becomes you less and less. Start biting on the lip!"

The femme reaching for the Garuda bird and rapping it sharply, startling even Marc.

In the diffusion, like a fade-in, the forming of a separate face. None other than a painted portrait of Miss Hudd and Sons, and ever worthy of a flutter of the heart.

"People," she said. "A pleasure. So unexpected."

Wouldn't it be lovely if it were?

Then, with caution; "What might I do for you?"

The femme: "Marc, as you see, is calling on his grand-mother, thank you."

Miss Hudd: "Witnessing open inspections of one's own home can be terminally bad for the nerves. She's miles away."

Marc: "I'm here. What about my nerves?"

The femme, raising the warning finger . . . "Very well, Miss Hudd, where do we find her?"

"That's your problem, I fear. I'm not in the market for any problems but my own. She regards her whereabouts as personal business."

The femme, with a sigh: "Marc has a long-standing appointment."

"I've heard about it. Three-thirty tomorrow."

"Three-thirty today, Miss Hudd."

Miss Hudd, with intensity: "Tomorrow. And not then, either." Her eyes fixing on Marc. "You'll have to face it. She had no serious intention of going through with this jaunt. I see no reason to protect you any longer. She was calling your mother this evening to put an end to it. Nothing about today, about your turning up here, has endeared you to anyone. The place for you is the next bus out. Finally, had you managed to equip yourself to bid at tomorrow's auction, you'd have got nowhere. Are you hearing me?"

Marc thinking: Whose throat do I cut? Hers or mine?

The femme: "I have a feeling the story we're hearing is avoiding certain points of interest."

"I wouldn't know what you're talking about."

"Then you'd surprise me."

"I have no authority to answer outsiders. Only to speak with Marc."

"I understand you warned Marc off this morning. You can't have it all ways."

Miss Hudd and Sons might have begun to look vulnerable. "You can't expect me to discuss business confidences. Nor can you seriously suggest that anyone has acted illegally. We're not rogues. We're not fools."

"Well, why have you gone to such lengths to keep it quiet?"

"Keep what quiet? You've inspected the property twice yourself."

"The family had no knowledge of the sale."

"What would you know about the family?"

"That's naïve, Miss Hudd."

"Information relating to the sale is conspicuously available. What does that suggest to you? I know what it suggests to me, and it doesn't say much for the family."

"Now you're making hurtful judgements on very little evidence."

"On more evidence than you think! From her point of view it was the boy. Constantly trying to spare him. *She's had a very difficult time.*"

"Others have had a difficult time, Miss Hudd. Mrs. Leadbeater has had many opportunities to break the news. Even yesterday. Even last night. Had Marc been told then, he might've been spared a great deal . . ."

"All days have been equally difficult in this respect. And did he bother to turn up himself? Even at the widely discussed three-thirty? His grandmother waiting for hours with his lunch and in a state of mind I'd hardly know how to explain."

Marc wanting to walk off into the sea as Gramps had done.

"You see him beside me," the femme said. "And did you not confront him hereabouts at around noon? But this becomes pointless, Miss Hudd, and wasteful of time. The police? What are they doing here?"

"Police business is police business."

"Where do we find them?"

"Outside. At the back. At last sighting."

"Thank you. May we pass through? Or do we apply for written permission?"

Miss Hudd and Sons losing much of her cutting edge. Becoming less visible, as if lights inside her were going out.

This cruel world that began when Gramps met his nemesis . . .

Marc not able to endure it without showing the glint of tears.

But he was taking the first feared step into the house, just the same, behind the femme, as if there had never been an alternative.

The first step across in months and months; a time like a weary plodding to this day; like a long, exhausting journey. Perhaps, mercifully, the floor might open and he might go on falling through for the rest of his life.

Marc attempting to give Miss Hudd and Sons one quick, wounded, sideways, farewell glance. Not knowing if she cared. Not knowing if she saw.

How can you look so nice and say such cruel things? Do you want to scar me all over? Here I am hoping never to see you again.

Into a house full of people he'd never met and didn't want to know. Full of people trampling on sacred things. Full of spent energies that others might have called ghosts.

Marc nervously a step behind the femme, shuffling, groping into an unreal place. As if his dream had become life. As if walls and ceilings were about to close in and crush him. Yet again catching the smell of the slow-drying oil painted by Gramps last Easter, only four or five days before he died. *Now she sells it.*

The surprisingly cold hand of the femme reaching back and drawing him past the painting and the group glimpsed from the open doorway. The several people there having gone silent, making a thing of making a way. As if fearing that chance contact with such matters of importance might bear badly upon them at the sale.

Suddenly, thankfully, out of the dark channel of the house, into the light of evening.

The patio. The garden. The Forsythe fence. And immediately no more firm grip of the femme's cold hand. But her voice firmer by far than he'd ever heard it.

"Sergeant Costello. Constable Davis. Good evening."

The voice of the sergeant: "Miss Campbell. Boy."

Abruptly: "His name is Marc."

"We've met."

Marc wondering why life had to become a tragedy. For so long so much of it had been a gentle comedy, even at its worst.

Marc trying to block it out with counting. Trying to fill his head with the noise of numbers. Numbers might bring Gramps down among them to take care of all these things.

The femme: "We share an anxiety, Marc and I. There's a misunderstanding with Mrs. Leadbeater."

"Is there? Tell me about it."

Here she was: the femme: her cloak of armour on; but answering the questions.

"Marc expected to meet his grandmother here. Yet the

story is that she expected him tomorrow. And the reality, we're told, was her intention not to meet him at all. You're aware of the terms of the grandfather's will?"

"Why's the lad not telling me this?"

"Because I insist that he shall not try."

"What are you to him?"

"It's what he is to me."

A shriek from Marc: "The Jag."

"Yes," said the sergeant. "The Jag."

"It's gone!"

"Correct. And curious. Hence our presence."

The femme: "Summoned by whom?"

The sergeant to the femme: "By Miss Hudd. When she opened up the house at 5:20, the Jaguar had gone. She called Mrs. Leadbeater at her other address, but there was no answer to the phone." Then to Marc: "We've been hoping you might assist us, having noted you were in town."

Marc brought up short. "What's *that* supposed to mean?"

The femme: "No matter how you feel about the question, you'll reply politely."

Marc biting on his lip. Clenching his fists . . .

The femme: "Under certain conditions, Sergeant—the prior death of Mrs. Leadbeater being one of them—this aged vehicle was to become Marc's own on his twenty-fifth birthday. Along with the balance of the estate."

"In an ideal world, Miss Campbell, these things might come to pass . . . As the boy is learning, such is not the nature of the world."

"If that ultimate misfortune should befall Mrs. Leadbeater prior to 11:00 a.m. tomorrow, the sale, of course, would be off."

"That could be called a provocative statement, Doctor."

Marc breaking in: "It had a flat tyre!"

"Yes. And a foot pump was used to inflate it. Tell me—you tell me—how you knew it was flat."

The femme giving Marc the nod with the raising of a cautionary finger.

"I saw it," Marc said, "along with the spiderwebs and all the muck and pluck. But I didn't make off with it and I don't see how anyone else could've."

"Nonetheless, someone did."

"So someone pumped up the tyre. And the battery worked. After sitting here all winter? Some battery!"

"Doesn't your grandmother use the car?"

"What's that got to do with it?"

"The use of the car, boy, charges the battery. Or another battery could've been introduced."

Marc grimacing. "Well, I've never seen her use it."

"Does she drive?"

"I wouldn't know."

"Why wouldn't you?"

The femme: "He has too much on his mind, Sergeant, to mess you around."

"I'd hope so. Especially out of working hours. I'd hate to be chasing goods still safely in the care of the family."

"The car is *not* in the care of the family!"

"Marc, I imagine he knows that."

"Doesn't sound like it to me. You tell him if he wants confirmation, he knows where he can get it! They watched me onto the place this morning and watched me off. As usual, sittin' on the fence like a couple of magpies."

Marc, with an arm in the air, forefinger flung in the direction of the Forsythe boundary, suddenly proclaiming in the manner of his grandfather: "The Jag and my Gran! In collusion! This is what it's all about, I'll bet you!"

"Collusion?" said the sergeant.

"Driving off into her sunset."

"In collusion?"

"Heading for Nemesis! Running out into the sea. Yelling, *Wait for me, wait for me.* Oh hell . . . Oh bloody hell . . ."

The femme: "I regret that it's constructive, Sergeant."

Marc short on breath: "The magpies. You ask them. You're the police. Whatever's happened round here, they'll know."

The sergeant addressing the constable: "It's not likely there's another car between here and Nemesis, but check." Giving the femme a frown. "All we've got of this is bare bone, but I gather you regard it as urgent?"

"Yes."

"Make your way to the gate. Unhurriedly, please. Giving me time to sound out the Forsythes. If they confirm, as the boy suggests, I'll be looking to you both to put some flesh on the bones. I don't like the sound of these bones."

SIXTEEN

———◆◆◆———

Leadbeater's
Last Stand

MARC AND the femme fatale waiting. As if for an amputation.

The femme silent. And tired. With a look that probably meant she'd gone farther than ever intended.

But Marc going back to counting seconds, again seeking sanctuary in sacred numbers. Trying to make blotting-out noises with them in his head. But stopping, capriciously (like Gramps), at a hundred and thirty-five.

"Ma'am, what's the fine for obstructing traffic with a stationary car?"

The femme giving him the clouded eye, as if viewing him from the remote side of misted spectacles. "Is this the time to produce vulgarities?"

"In my opinion, ma'am, all due respect, no vulgarity intended, you could save yourself a hundred and thirty-five lovely dollars if you got out there and parked closer to the kerb. Making a nice, clean, expeditious job of it."

"In my opinion, Marc, you'd be better employed boiling your head."

"Only trying to keep you solvent, ma'am. Being some-
what in your debt and in no position to pay the fine on
your behalf. Which, if I were a man of property, I might
well insist on, prior to taking you out for a slap-up feed at
the Captain Cook or Sebastiano's."

"I've no intention of fooling around in the middle of a
street inhabited by police spies. The car is admirably placed
for a quick getaway."

"Many a word proud in jest, ma'am . . . One quick twist
of the key and I'll blend your wreck with the landscape.
No one'll ever see it again. To the general raising of tone
of the district. And with luck, you won't find it again yourself. Then you can spend your money at Gertrude's on low-
fat lunches instead of giving it to the law or the panel
beater."

Her reply had something to do with underskilled, over-
confident, undereducated, unlicensed teenagers driving under the noses of hawk-eyed police sergeants, and where did
he imagine that might put him?

But Marc losing the trend, for entering by the gateway,
a family, with an excited squeak from its midst: "Is this
really, *really*, the house we're going to have?"

Children dragging on the adults, dragging them in. Like
a rush of young horses. Four children at least. Five—if
Marc recklessly included the grown girl among the squeak-
ers, as Marc found himself caught with a pain. Then pinned
by a voice that said: *"Look who's here. See how I take care
of you. Don't let her get away again."*

The girl with the hair. The girl with the eyes. Her lips
parting for her own moment of surprise. Her head inclining
towards Marc, as everything within him, heart and soul,
was inclining towards her.

Hello there, he said to the pain inside. Hello, you. Oh,

would you believe! For she'd gone again, as before, among a crush of others, beyond reach or attainment. Leaving the same questions: Were her eyes blue or hazel or green? Even if her hair, for a moment, still remained to be seen. Dark hair? Fair hair? In between? But at heart who cared? Except to remember her by.

"Marc . . ."

A soft call from the femme: "Who is she?"

Marc hearing himself in the distance: "Only a dream, ma'am."

"Doesn't need to be. I saw her. And she saw you. As real as real could be."

Marc boyishly twisting his mouth, boyishly avoiding her eyes, but gladly taking a grip of her hand. How cold it was still.

"Confidentially, ma'am, I think I could go for you. Sort of somewhere between Miss Gorgeous—on her best days—and my delectable Rosemary, with a dash of my mum for sanity."

"That's sweet of you, Marc, though I don't know where it leaves me."

Marc sniffing and managing an expressive flicker of the nostrils.

"How would I have coped with today? What would I have done on my own? What was it you said about the sale being off?"

But his eyes turning to the house. The girl had gone on into the shadows of the verandah. Gone on and farther in.

She'd smell the oils so slow to dry. She'd see the picture the oils had made. And then she'd know about Marc.

"Are you sure you wouldn't like me to move your car and save you all those lovely dollars?"

"Certain."

"We could have a right royal spread on the savings."

"I don't know when . . ."

Might the girl return to the edge of the verandah as if to view the garden or the sunset?

Marc then said, "I don't suppose Gran *has* to have the Jag. Someone could've pinched it. I don't suppose it *has* to be her, crushed under some truck by now or wrapped around some tree. That's what you mean, isn't it? If she kills herself, the sale's off because that'd mean the property had come to me."

"It doesn't *have* to be her, Marc. As you say."

"What are they playin' at, then? These police? Why don't they come? Are they cooking dinner or something? She could be hurtling along at a hundred miles an hour, not knowing how to stop. She could be flopping round in the surf. She could be doing a hundred stupid things. *Don't leave me*, she was crying to him in that terrible dream. *Marcus, wait for me*. Talk about high drama in a fit. If I were a film I'd be banned."

"I remind you, Marc . . . kindly. That your dream wasn't real life. Wasn't on the six o'clock news. It was a fable. It was your own unconscious mind manipulating matters that have got out of hand."

"Do you reckon, ma'am? Is that why you tried to start your car with the key to the bathroom? Or whatever key it was. Is that why you rushed me round here on two wheels as if everyone's life was falling off the edge?"

She allowed it to pass.

"But if it's dark before we're there, what then? Have you had an eyeful of those cliffs? Have you seen the track we'd be taking down? Have you seen those waves screaming up the beach bent on ironing the continent flat?"

The femme appeared to have become excessively tired.

"It's a wonderful place," she said. "Very beautiful. You're not the only person in the world who's learnt to fear it."

"I don't see anything beautiful. It's a shockin' place. Get us out of it. Take us home. All that lovely food going to waste. Us dyin' to get stuck into it."

"Lovely once, Marc. Hardly worth it now."

The sergeant: "She had a service van from the Royal Auto Club at 4:46. They got the Jaguar on the road at 5:04. She drove off alone and turned left at the north end. In every way appearing to be competent."

Marc: "She couldn't be . . ."

"Nemesis Beach. Is there anywhere else in that direction she had a liking for?"

Marc crying: "How the hell would I know? I can hardly believe she can drive at all. Where else but Nemesis? The big splash. Gramps and his twin exhausts. Gramps and his foot to the floor. Gran playing the big melodrama to the one-man gallery of me, for reasons known only to her."

"I like that, boy. That's saying something. But are you saying the right things? Would they allow her through? Would they ever let her in?"

"She'd get through the same way as the rest of us. With the same permit. It's stuck to the windscreen. Signed by some bigwig in the Defence Department."

"Careless of your grandfather, sticking matters like that where they shouldn't be. Let's get moving, then. Casting, as you go, a grateful nod in the direction of the Forsythes. One of life's ironies, boy. Without their confirmation, you could've been stuck here half the night while we were putting things together."

Marc in despair clinging to the femme's hand. Draining her strength. In greater and greater need.

The sergeant: "You'll both come with us. We've noted your alignment with the kerb, Doctor. You're having another of your bad days. Give the key to the constable and he'll make it legal. Courtesy of the department."

Marc in a daze.

The sergeant, now on duty at the rear door of the patrol car. Precise and gentle. "Come along."

Marc following on after the femme. Hearing the door close. Feeling its impact of air.

Knowing he was in. Knowing he was committed. Not knowing to what.

In a few moments movement, and the mirrored reflections of flashing blue lights across the enraptured faces of the Smut Society and the Forsythes.

But everyone could have done without the siren.

"Turn it off, Constable! Or I'll have your head."

Marc Leadbeater, a few crowded moments to himself:

Here we go. Dark for sure. As if I didn't know.

Haven't I seen it in the stars? Standing outside with the frost in the air, sensing him everywhere.

You watch me go over the edge. Arms and legs. Tumbling over and down. Out of sight of all. Though I'll hear them way back there yelling my name as I run down the sand.

A pity about the girl with the eyes. A pity about Delectable. A pity about the femme. A pity about all these women in my life. You never know, do you, where things like it could end?

I'll be calling, "Gran, Gran." Whether she's there, or stuck in some car yard doing a deal, or having steak and eggs somewhere.

Here comes destiny, Rudolphus Blickenwicker. Whoever you are. You and your mum singing her songs in her

*G-string. You and your three lessons a week from Miss
What's-her-name.*

Looks like you people have got it made.

*I remind you gods up there swinging your legs from your
clouds, I'm not seventy-four. I'm sixteen.*

The moment of truth.

Police car closing on a point of glare that threw bars of
brilliance and blackness across the roadway and the forest
trees.

Marc so sore from the pain of his breathless briefing of
the sergeant that he feared he'd be sick in his own lap.

The femme silent again, as if the strain and the briefing
had been too much.

A roadblock. A guardhouse. A soldier with a weapon.

The car braking, throwing Marc into the pressure of the
seat belt, all but turning his stomach, his hand going to his
mouth.

The femme calming him. Oh, she was a good girl.

Outside, an illuminated sign:

DEPARTMENT OF DEFENCE
PROHIBITED AREA
DO NOT PASS

The year of signs. St. Sign's Day. Everybody with a sign.
I'll wear one myself, thought Marc, hung about my neck:

MARCUS LEADBEATER XVI
ONCE LIVED HERE

The sentry crisply: "Dip your headlights!"

The sergeant: "Constable, you heard the nice man."

"You have business," said the sentry, "with whom?"

The sergeant, leaning across: "I have business with everybody in due course. You'll recall your own last New Year's Eve."

Marc at the edge of his seat.

"I inquire," said the sergeant, "(a) as to why you do not answer your phone, and (b) after a steel-grey Jaguar Mark II, 1963, driven by a lady, with departmental permit of entry stuck to the windscreen. Have you admitted the lady in the last hour?"

"The answer to (a), Sergeant Costello, is that the phone hasn't rung. And the answer to (b) is yes."

Marc slumping back against the femme.

"Has the lady returned?"

"No, Sergeant Costello."

"Are you perturbed that she hasn't?"

"It was Mrs. Leadbeater. Widow of the professor. The car he always drove. Everything was in order, Sergeant Costello."

"I'm sure it was. Tell me more."

"She said it was an occasion. A farewell."

I can hear her, Marc thought, as if I'd actually heard her.

"She said she was going away. She'd like an hour or two. I referred to the Officer of the Guard."

"Well done. Kindly refer to him again."

Marc labouring for breath. Internally cold. The femme's hand almost warm by comparison.

Marc still hunting for thoughts to block out other things. Almost thankful he might never have to be a soldier. Imagine being a sentry at a place like this. Poor fellow. Having to deal with Costello.

The brisk presence of the Officer of the Guard.

"Sergeant Costello."

"Lieutenant."

"What has Mrs. Leadbeater to do with you?"

A backward flick of the sergeant's hand. "Her grandson on the left. Dr. Campbell on the right. Both have passed this point with Leadbeater, deceased, in happier days. We believe Mrs. Leadbeater is disturbed. Your Surf Rescue Squad might do worse than follow us down at the double."

"The day's done," said the Officer of the Guard. "We're not on a war footing here, Sergeant. They're off duty."

"So am I. But you're not. I take it I may proceed?"

SEVENTEEN

Leadbeater in Total

MARC UNCOMMONLY uneasy and unsure about the company he was keeping. Arriving at a sense of having been dismantled and in need of parts. As if components of himself had been removed by force.

Yet he was getting where he needed to be. No denying it. He was at the edge of it, the moment of truth, or of falsehood, and of whatever else. Though still arrested by the restraint of the femme's hand, placed firmly over his, both remaining cold.

Coldness like hers had to mean something, and he doubted that it meant good.

Marc shaking his head with many doubts. Doubts, even, about whose side she was on. And suffering, in consequence, the wrong kind of palpitations about it. Down in the pit of his stomach, where it shortened his breath again and made him queasy again.

Not long since she'd been saying his moment was waiting for him. And adding that he'd not be facing it alone.

Lady, you were introducing the conflict even then. You'd

dropped your guard. Your slip was showing. I was too thick in the skull to spot it.

If I don't face my moment alone, ma'am, it's not my moment.

Elementary mathematics, as someone we know would have said.

You people have been getting at me. You police and my lovely femme. Telling me to be a good boy. To stay put. To twiddle my thumbs. Not to move. To leave everything that needs to be done to the mercy of the competent ones. By interpretation this means I get ruled out of taking part in my own big scene. A scene, I say, as personal as getting born!

Name me another that'll stand alongside it. You'll be battling. You can't go past dicing with the risk of gettin' unborn—this moment lying out there now, I reckon, over the edge like some giant clam itching to snap shut.

Is that where Gramps, the dope, has ended up getting himself stuck?

Holed up with the sea-serpent for the rest of time inside some bloody great clam?

A determined change in Marc. A change of mind and heart.

Starting on the fatigue. The haze of it and the maze of it. The dragging tiredness of spirit that hour by hour and minute by minute had worn him down. Now hauling himself back up through it. While, outside, the headlight beams were groping along the high edges of the cliff, casting alarming shadows, but revealing nothing he couldn't have written high, wide, and handsome across the windscreen a week in advance.

Marc still palpitating, deeply resenting that his lovely

lady was treating him like the kid being sick on the ferry on his tenth birthday. She'd joined with the police to block the course of his life.

Was that why she was cold? Because she didn't go much for what she was doing? And cared about it? And worried about it? Or was just plain scared about it?

Marc tugging to free his hand.

The femme hanging on.

What's done is done, Gramps used to say. Done, like the sum added up. Inferring, my boy, by logical extension, that what is to be shall be. Like the answer to the sum still to be added up . . .

Well, that was our Gramps. The religious heretic. The mathematical saint. The jester—if you were quick enough and cute enough to pick it up.

Marc breathing hard and fast. For a second or two seeing himself again as the traveller who had lost his little piece of paper of the relevant colour. But blanking it off with defiance, for in the end had he not found it? Screwed up. In the last corner of the last hip pocket.

Marc pressing his anger close. Cuddling it.

Engine of the police car cutting. Wheel ruts in deep pine bark vanishing. Headlights damping out. Blackness, as if in an instant they had plunged over the edge a mile underground.

Marc shaking.

Was there a hard-gut expulsion of breath from the front seat? Was this the *ultimate* cliff? Well, it had to be. The very edge of it. The concrete blocks. The wheel stops. Was that the Jaguar alongside? Like condensation on an early-morning windowpane?

All such things, without the need of sight, to Marc being known in the instant of jerking into revolt.

Breaking the femme's grasp. Like taking freedom bought at a price.

Throwing open the door. Meeting open air. Meeting the cold. Leaping into the wind.

Friends, Romans, countrymen, clear the decks . . .

Somewhere the rumble and roar of masses of water meeting the shore. Somewhere down there the hearty breakfast for the happy condemned.

I'll take it, I say, if I must. Have it ready. Have it hot.

Sky out in front and all around, vivid in the startling vision of the savage sixteen-year-old. Darkness and afterglow. Black holes and supernovae. Those legions of angels on their night out painting the town redder than ever, spilling their wine into the sea below.

RUN!

I'm running, man.

Marc eluding their hands. Delivering the elbow lunge sharply to each side.

To you, ma'am, I say sorry for each hurt, BUT NOW'S THE TIME.

"Stop him!"

Running with eyes in his knees. Away from strong flashlight beams pursuing like outstretched arms. Marc running from memory and from instinct, and launching himself over the edge, for this was the descent shared with his lovely Gramps since time began.

Carried in the arms of Gramps. Or clinging to his hand. Or skipping a step behind. Or rushing on ahead, tripping, leaving Gramps yelling back there, "For God's sake, boy, take care. Do you want to scare me to death?"

But never before without Gramps.

Never before alone.

Now the shock of stumbles on crude steps of sandstone,

breaking edges striking back to the nape of his neck. And strips of deep sliding sand all but pulling him down. And the jolt of eroded gaps jarring even to his teeth. All spilling underfoot like sand in an hourglass with a minute to run.

Faintly heard: "Constable. Where the hell's he gone? What the hell's he done?"

A cry from the femme. Like the final illumination of a last brushstroke. Like a parting gesture from an actor not written in by the playwright.

The femme then no more to be heard. No more ever to be heard? Or to be seen? Like the best page of all carried off on a gust of wind.

Interludes come, Gramps used to say, and go.

(There being nothing about which he had nothing to say.)

Interludes being made of the stuff that one gets over, my boy. That one recovers from. Then puts aside. Though they give us the shape of what others believe us to be.

Marc missing his way. Floundering through vegetation. Falling. For the moment without comment, not even an oath.

Marc, the accident-prone. The kid with the strips of bandage and the plaster casts. The allergy kid. The one with the wheezes and the sneezes. Running true to form.

The oath. Shrieked.

Throwing out his arms in all directions. Generated from sixteen years of continuing experience. A form of evolutionary compensation for being born clumsy. At least four arms ever-ready for throwing out. Though five would not have surprised. Snatching at sharp or rough or breaking ends that came away with his numerous hands. Instantly drawing blood from each. Striking heaven only knew what with every available surface of his material self. Back, front, middle, bottom, top. Even with sensitive areas on the inner side.

I'll be red. I'll be blue. I'll be all the usual shades of black.

When you bail out, Gramps used to say, relax.

Have faith in your parachute, boy, unless you've packed it yourself.

Is there anything around here, Marc asked, that I've actually packed myself? This *has* to be the situation pre-packed by the experts.

Marc motionless, more or less, snatching a short interval to reflect.

I've arrived at Nemesis.

Methinks.

Which, for the moment, must leave me close to death. Or partly distant from life for a more practical death to be enjoyed later, at length. Or might it suggest an outbreak of immortality. Interesting concept. The first Marcus Leadbeater to be the permanent survivor. The first to whom no conquest might be considered beyond the norm.

The gods on their clouds finally pressing the panic button.

"Ye gods," cry the goddesses in particular, "an immortal Leadbeater. Let's do him in quick. Let's strike him down before the scandals of the classics, to which we have accustomed ourselves, require to be recast in phrases more compromising than formerly. Who feels equal to making a deadly lightning flash?"

Marc sighing and sitting up.

"Gran, I hope you're good and handy. We need to get this over good and quick."

True, I don't have the feel of being dead. Though I bet

I look it. The walking dead. If walking is a viable alternative to remainin' here as a kind of sign at the crossroads.

All my toes wiggle. All my fingers work. My spine doesn't
crackle in the middle.

"Do you hear me, Gran?"

Marc going through the motions; tottering onto his feet;
filling his lungs for a hefty shout.

*"I'd like you to come across, Gran, real soon. We've got
things to discuss."*

Deafer than everybody's favourite post. It must be catching. Like other problems of close relationships.

Well, here I am, even if she's not. Home and dry. Except
for tears of fright and gushing blood. Me favourite place
never to be found alive or dead. So be of good cheer, my
brothers and sisters of the greater communion, you could
be at home protecting your investments from multi-fingered
siblings or the pained investigations of your mum. Who's
always about to leave for morning coffee or afternoon tea
at the Foreign Aid Club. Or from the scrutiny of your dad,
the eye in the sky, looking dourly down over the total length
of his noble nose; if not hung up somewhere in London
Town nursing a virus or resting his pilot's elbow. And who
can doubt the word of the sinless man whom she trusts in
cities of noted ill repute? Darwin never had him in mind
when he wrote *The Descent of Man.* All the lovely sinful
bits being handed down intact by my lovely Gramps to me.

"Gran! For pity's sake, give us a hoy!"

Don't tell me she was in the Jag. Don't tell me we passed
her by. I couldn't *stand* it if she was sittin' there knittin'
and watching the moon come up.

And don't dare tell me that looking all filmy and feminine
and sweet sixteen, she's out there already making a play
for her old man.

Marc taking off down the sands, shedding everything short of his pants, glancing back to flashlight beams coming down the cliff like a regiment of illuminated stilts.

The army, allegedly, being off duty. But a mere three pairs of hands with flashlights, my brethren, never made a showing like that.

"Gran, we've got a crisis. Answer me, for God's sake."

Lights flooding the sands.

"BLOODY HELL."

Points of brilliance. Points of glare. Almost stopping his heart. Beaming from the face of the cliff. From poles or pylons on the bluffs lying west and east. All lit up like a city street. The whole wide world bent on cutting him off.

Marc swinging savagely into the south, into the sea that could have been an endless wall of glistening black. Onto the decline of shocking contours of sand and rock, the like of which, in any light, he'd never seen until this moment of shock.

"You silly bloody fool!"

Gran. On the sand. A mere fifty metres down, or less. Limp. Sprawled. Prostrated. Dying. Drowned. One or another. Streams of sea rushing back around her and across the top.

A world gone mad over the edges. Or was it always thus?

Marc crying, running, flying.

I've held all I can stand. I'll burst. I'll bust.

And letting go with his cry at its pitch. Stumbling on past. Losing direction. Landing heavily in the wet on his knees and the top of his head and outflung hands.

A body of driftwood, for God's sake, with limbs of kelp. No one's grandmother. No one's mother. No one's sister. No one's delectable mate. No sound either, of any consequence, only water, an enormous weight, rolling him over and swirling him and sweeping him into a slurry of seaweed and sand and God knows what else.

I'll be damned, Marc said. The sea-serpent.

Who has me heading, without a doubt, for the deep face down and leads me to ask, "Where'd you come from, you bloody great wave, serving no notice, begging no pardons, you accessory to the fact?"

I wasn't aimin' on bein' relegated just yet. So step aside, all you barracudas and rocks. My current and serious calculations have not included getting scrunched. I point out, surprised by the necessity, that what I've uttered lyrically, on the spur or stress of this moment or that, must be regarded as boyish misuse of long-established poetic principles and on no account to be taken seriously. I've never been dead keen on sea-serpents and bloody great clams, as is widely known, or on bloody great waves as culpable as this. Back where I come from, waves like you get locked up. Life's never been so frightful that I've ever been in the market for any alternative except bliss. What a loss to the human race. All my genius going down the chute, never blossoming on the bough, Wackenblicker scooping up the lot. Mixed metaphors! Oh my gosh. Miss G. She'll get me for that.